"Look out!" Janice shouted.

At a highway intersection, a midnight-blue SUV ignored a red light and roared toward her side of the lightweight car. Shane's plunge on the accelerator plastered Janice to her seat.

His face shrouded under the bill of a wide-brimmed hat, the driver of the other vehicle laid on his horn. The blast rang in Janice's ears as the little Ford whizzed beyond the SUV's massive bumper.

Sucking a quavering breath into her lungs, Janice stared at Shane's sober profile. His Adam's apple bobbed as he kept his gaze locked on the road.

"Did you notice a license plate number?" he asked.

"I was too scared, and it happened so fast."

She stared warily out the window at passing traffic. This was too weird. Was the whole island warning her away?

She'd left the family name and all such associations behind long ago, but did someone with a vendetta against the Morans know who she was? Unfortunately, the number of people with reason to hate the Morans—any Moran—was legion.

Did that include Shane Gillum?

Books by Jill Elizabeth Nelson

Love Inspired Suspense

Evidence of Murder
Witness to Murder
Calculated Revenge
Legacy of Lies
Betrayal on the Border
Frame-Up
Shake Down

JILL ELIZABETH NELSON

writes what she likes to read—faith-based tales of adventure seasoned with romance. By day she operates as housing manager for a seniors' apartment complex. By night she turns into a wild and crazy writer who can hardly wait to jot down all the exciting things her characters are telling her, so she can share them with her readers. More about Jill and her books can be found at www.jillelizabethnelson.com. She and her husband live in rural Minnesota, surrounded by the woods and prairie and their four grown children, who have settled nearby.

SHAKE DOWN

JILL ELIZABETH NELSON

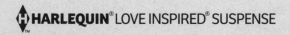

HARLEQUIN® LOVE INSPIRED® SUSPENSE

Recycling programs
for this product may
not exist in your area.

LOVE INSPIRED BOOKS

ISBN-13: 978-0-373-44607-0

SHAKE DOWN

www.Harlequin.com

Printed in U.S.A.

A good name is more desirable than great riches;
To be esteemed is better than silver or gold.
—*Proverbs* 22:1

With prayers of compassion for the victims of crime...and for the secondary victims— the innocent families of the guilty.

ONE

Janice Swenson squatted on her haunches, frowning down into the ink-black hole beneath a hatch in the floor. Dank air wafted into her face and she shivered. It was too easy to imagine this whole property rotting beneath the weight of fetid family secrets.

Disposing of this cottage she'd inherited from a distant relative might prove to be more troublesome than Janice would have anticipated. At any other time in her life, she'd have sold the property, sight-unseen, and called it good riddance. But she had her reasons for coming to Martha's Vineyard to handle the transaction personally.

If her superstitious days weren't well behind her, Janice might be tempted to think Moran Cottage was bent on doing her in. At her first step onto the front porch, she had nearly plunged her foot through an eroded board. Then as she'd explored the walk-in kitchen pantry, a shelf let loose, tumbling expired canned goods onto her shoulders. A few aches across her back betrayed bruises forming. Now she'd wrestled open a trap door in the floor of the hallway outside the miniscule bathroom and found the cellar.

At least her decade of experience as a Realtor had prepared her to deal with little issues such as lack of power in a run-down property. Janice swiped a flashlight from her belt-loop clip, clicked it on and pointed the beam into the pit. A set of treacherously steep stairs ended in a packed-earth floor.

She frowned. If she wanted to sell this unexpected—and unwanted—inheritance, besides adding onto the bathroom and completely renovating the kitchen, she might have to invest in pouring cement down here. Those projects would eat up a lot of her budget, making it doubly important that she do as much as she could of the simpler tasks herself—basic cleaning, wall-painting, buffing and refinishing the vintage wood floors and brightening up trim and moldings.

The plank steps appeared thick and sturdy, though the pitch of the descent was almost like a ladder's. Surely there was another entrance from outside the cottage, probably a set of those nearly flat-to-the-ground cellar doors, but why traipse through the overgrown weeds outside when access lay before her?

Janice hauled in a cleansing breath and squared her shoulders. If snakes or spiders lurked below, she might be startled for a split second, but she could thank God neither arachnophobia nor ophidiophobia numbered among her issues.

With one hand on the adjacent wall, she lowered herself and found the top step solid, though the nails emitted small creaks that echoed faintly through the darkness. She continued her descent until her head dipped below the floor then panned her flashlight around the space that yawned like a man-made cavern. Square, oaken pillars, similar to the ones that held up the porch roof, supported the floor above in strategic places. The area seemed to be as large as the entire cabin and to have no interior walls, but the flashlight beam didn't penetrate far enough to tell.

Could she turn this space into another living area? She'd have to find a better light source to make that decision. There must be an overhead lightbulb with a string, or even a light switch, down here. It would be nice to know where it was for when the power company turned on the electricity later today—provided its staff kept their promise.

Peering intently into the shadows, hunting for that elusive bulb or light switch, Janice lowered herself onto the next step.

Crack!

The board collapsed beneath her foot, pitching her forward. A scream rent her throat and her flashlight flew away as her hands thrust out instinctively to catch her fall. She hadn't far to go, but far enough for impact with the hard-as-cement earthen floor to rattle every bone in her body. Bright pain speared up her left arm.

Janice lay flat on her stomach, fighting breath into her lungs and groping for a coherent thought. *Stupid!* She'd become distracted and forgot to pay attention to the conditions in an unfamiliar environment.

Tears filled her eyes and she whimpered as she gingerly gathered herself into a sitting position. Heat banded her left wrist and she hugged the arm to her chest. *Great!* Now she was injured—whether a sprain or a break had yet to be determined. Either condition could incapacitate her for weeks, and she'd allowed herself only the summer to finish the work, sell the place and shake off the muck of family legacy. This time forever.

Janice collected her flashlight and hooked it to her belt loop. Then she struggled to her knees, and from there, to her feet. One knee stung, but at least no other body part seemed to have suffered more than minor abrasions and bruises. Biting her lower lip between her teeth, she cautiously started up the steep stairs. The third from the bottom step had given way where it would have been fastened to the side panels. Those creaky nail sounds took on new significance.

With a soft moan, she lifted her leg high over the missing step and finally managed to emerge onto the main floor hallway. As much as she would have liked to slide down the wall, huddle on the dusty floor and indulge in a good cry, she forced herself to head up the passage.

Her rental car sat in the weed-infested gravel parking area beside the cottage. The drive from here to the hospital, shaken and hurting, didn't appeal to her, but neither did calling for an ambulance—if cell service even existed out here.

She rounded the corner into the main room, empty of furnishings like the rest of the cottage. Movement outside the mullioned picture window stopped her in her tracks. Her jaw gaped as oxygen vacated her lungs.

Someone stood on the porch, face framed in a rectangular pane. In the shade of the porch roof, she couldn't make out features, but the dark craters that must be eyes fixed her with molten intensity. She'd never been one to sense emotion from people the way her psychologist friend Laurel did, but the sheer malice of the glare wrapped Janice in a sheet of ice. So this is what people meant when they said their blood ran cold.

"Who—who's there?" She forced the words past rigid lips.

The porch boards moaned as the figure tromped away. By an act of will, Janice wobbled out the door in pursuit. Trespasser or not, surely she'd imagined the ill intent. Maybe this person would help her get to the hospital. If not, she'd at least like to be able to describe the intruder if she decided to report the incident to the authorities.

Avoiding the rotten board, Janice crossed the porch and trod down the front steps. A tangy Atlantic breeze billowed through her windbreaker and tossed a veil of chestnut hair across her face. With an exasperated huff, she used her good hand to brush the long strands behind her ear. She should have bound up the unruly mop in a ponytail this morning.

Where had the person gone?

Her gaze spotted no intruder scampering down the hillside strewn with boulders and tufts of greening vegetation. At the bottom of the incline, the slim ribbon of white beach lay empty except for small rocks glinting like grayish marbles amidst shiny granules of fine sand. The playful tussle between surf and sand made a chuckling, shushing sound as sunbeams danced on lacy blue waves as far as the eye could see. The sights and sounds would be calming if she weren't in pain and alarmed by an intruder.

Clutching her throbbing wrist, she started a cautious circuit of the cottage. If someone was there she'd easily see the person. Moran Cottage poked up from the ground like an impudent blip on ten acres of overgrown pastureland. Though the cottage came with a shed and, of all things, a functional outhouse, the nearest inhabited structure lay beyond a distant stand of oak and maple trees.

At the side entrance to the kitchen, Janice climbed up pitted cement steps and tried the door, but found it locked. At least a vandal or a robber would have to break something to get in. Like the front window? What would the intruder have done if he hadn't caught sight of her? Was the trespasser merely curious or bent on mayhem?

She moved to the rear of the cottage. Still no one. The pastureland stretched barren and empty. The outhouse was vacant and the shed was locked up tight—no hiding place there. A little farther up the back of the cottage, she found the outside cellar entrance. A rusty chain and enormous, aging padlock secured the doors. She'd need chain cutters to gain access unless the key to the old lock was somewhere among the jumble of antique furnishings and outright junk stored in a rental facility in Edgartown.

Sighing, she scanned the open field once more. Surely a trespasser wouldn't have had time to get out of sight. Had

her senses been addled by the fall so that her mind con-
cocted from thin air the person at her window?

She plodded to the front of the cottage and up the porch
steps. Gingerly finding her way over the treacherous board,
she pulled her key ring from her jeans' pocket. She needed
to lock up and get to the only island hospital as best she
could on her own.

Deep barks erupted from the beach area and Janice
turned around. A mottled-brown dog the size of a small
pony romped in a circle around a tall man who strolled
along the edge of the surf. His attention was on the ocean,
not on the cottage or on her.

"Hey!" Janice cried, waving her good arm in the air.

Her stomach lurched with a twinge of queasiness in
reaction to prolonged pain. It was definitely a good idea
to recruit help in reaching the hospital emergency room.

"Hey!" she hollered again and tottered off the porch,
still waving.

The dog halted and let out staccato woofs as it stared
in her direction. The animal's master said something to it,
though Janice couldn't make out what. Then the man lifted
a hand toward her and trotted up the faint path between the
beach and the cottage, dog loping at his side. A gray An-
orak hugged his broad shoulders, and long legs clad in a
pair of faded jeans easily conquered the steep hillside. The
wind ruffled thick sandy-brown hair above a broad smile.

"Hello," the man called from yards away. "Shane Gillum here. And this is Atlas." He patted the top of the dog's
head. "You must be my new neighbor."

"I'm hurt," Janice said. "Can you—"

Dizziness swept through her and she staggered back
against the porch rails. A snap sounded from the roof overhang and the dog let out a sharp bark.

"Watch it!" Shane yelled, breaking into a run toward her.

A blow hammered the top of Janice's head. Pain enveloped her skull as the sky and landscape waxed a midnight-blue shot with sparkly pinpoints of light. Then nothing.

Lips pressed into a tight line, Shane knelt beside the woman sprawled on the ground and checked the pulse at the graceful curve of her throat. Strong and steady. That much was good. Cursory examination of the wound buried beneath thick reddish-brown hair revealed a superficial cut. An amount of blood welled from the injury out of proportion to the size of the trauma—typical of head wounds—but the cleansing blood flow was already tapering off. He wouldn't touch the site and risk infection.

However, serious injury to the skull might lurk beneath the minor cut. Shane peeled back the lids of her eyes. The pupils were of matching and normal size inside vivid green irises. Uniform pupils were another good sign, but it was too soon to become complacent. He needed to get her to a medical facility as quickly as possible.

Just before that chunk of roofing tile crashed onto her head, hadn't she said something about being injured? Even while she was speaking to him, she'd staggered. Was one of her legs hurt?

Shane scanned the tall and slender yet very feminine length of the woman's body. She wore a dirt-smudged blue windbreaker over a gray sweatshirt, a pair of sensible sneakers and designer jeans—expensive, unless he missed his guess—sporting a coat of dust and a small rent in the knee that looked recent and not a part of the design. He skimmed his hands down one leg and then the other. No discernible swelling.

At his side, Atlas whined. Shane ruffled the bristly fur at the dog's neck.

"It'll be all right, boy." Hopefully he spoke the truth. "This wasn't the way we'd planned to meet the new owner of Moran Cottage, if it came to it, eh?"

Not by a long shot. He'd hoped against hope no one would bother to put in an appearance until his business at the cottage was done, but he'd been prepared for worse to come to worst. Depending on who showed up at the property, he'd considered everything from becoming some crotchety battle-ax's right-hand man to the role of indispensable island guide to a pasty-faced office drone. That he might be confronted with a model-stunning woman around his own age hadn't featured in his imagination.

Would he have to stoop to romancing a Moran? Bile rose in his throat.

Maybe this chance to act the hero would prove a blessing in disguise…as long as his own disguise remained intact. Shane's teeth clenched. Getting close to the heir was his last shot at unearthing the records that would restore his family's honor. Of course, under normal circumstances he'd help any injured soul without a second thought—was trained to do so. A Moran, however, he'd be tempted to let rot.

The woman groaned and his heart jerked. She was coming around.

Shane yanked his cell phone from his belt pouch to request emergency services, but naturally found no signal. Despite the best efforts of a variety of cellular companies, dead areas were prevalent on the island.

Expelling hot air through his nose, Shane holstered his phone and rose to his feet. He scanned the area for the woman's mode of transportation. If she'd driven out here on one of those tourist-popular rental motorbikes, he'd have to go all the way back to his leased cabin a quarter mile away to get his Jeep.

But the bumper of a compact car jutted from the side of the cottage. What were the chances she'd left the keys in the vehicle, along with the handbag she wasn't carrying?

Shane took a step toward the car and his foot trod on

a chunk of the roof tile that had fallen. The tile bore his weight without crumbling, not a sign consistent with frail material. Wearing a frown, he bent and picked up the slice of thick red slate. The piece looked considerably newer than the building, though minor pitting indicated enough age to have been on the roof for a couple of decades. No cracks or faults marred the surface or the broken edge.

In his uneducated opinion, the break should have appeared smooth, though not necessarily straight. Instead, regular striations along three-quarters of the broken edge suggested some kind of tool. A small saw?

Every muscle tensed as he gazed across the unfenced pastureland, but he spotted no lurker. What did he expect? A saboteur standing around gawking at the results of his handiwork?

Shane returned his attention to the evidence of tampering. Apparently someone else had a vendetta against the Morans. Given the family history, that hardly came as a surprise.

Or maybe the sabotage was directly connected to Shane's search. Could his enemies be privy to the information that had sent him here incognito? A chill seeped through him. Was this falling roof tile intended for him and not the injured woman at his feet? Was she innocent of complicity?

Shane snorted. An innocent Moran? The phrase was an oxymoron.

And why mask deliberate mayhem in the guise of an accident? The approach didn't fit the modus operandi of a crime family that thought nothing of snuffing out the life of anyone who crossed them. Twice now, a hit man's bullet had nearly added Shane to the dead list, prompting him to change his name, alter his appearance and acquire a dog—a pet his true self would never have possessed.

Shane glanced at the Italian Griffin sniffing delicately at the woman on the ground.

She was truly lovely. Too bad she was neck deep in intrigue she might not know existed. His pulse stumbled through several beats then his jaw hardened to granite. *God, You don't play fair!* Now, not only must he keep himself among the living, but he was forced to protect a Moran long enough to uncover the truth.

TWO

Fetid breath fanned Janice's cheeks. Someone needed a date with a toothbrush. She opened her eyes and a bewhiskered face with enormous brown eyes filled her vision. A long red tongue flicked out and swiped the tip of her nose.

With a gasp, Janice sat up and scuttled backward. Pain swooped through her skull and jabbed her injured wrist. The dog with the uncannily human face yelped and scurried over to his master who stood examining one of the roof tiles that must have crashed down on her head.

How many "accidents" did Moran Cottage have in store for her? Were they accidents? Surely they must be. But the intruder— She shook her head and winced at the responding throb. Her brain was too fuzzy to sort this out right now.

"Take it easy, ma'am," said the man. "Atlas won't hurt you."

What had this guy said his name was? Shane—that was it. If she wasn't experiencing so much as a millisecond of memory loss from the head blow, maybe she wasn't in as bad shape as she felt.

"I'm not scared of the dog, Shane. I like animals. He just startled me. I'm Janice Swenson, by the way."

"Pleased to meet you, Janice Swenson. I wish the circumstances were better." Shane knelt on one knee in front of her. Sea-blue eyes dissected her. "Where are you injured—other than your head?"

"My arm." She clutched the throbbing limb to her chest. "I fell down the cellar stairs."

"Ouch!" His wince breathed sympathy. "May I see?"

Something about his air of competence drew obedience from Janice, and she trapped a moan behind clenched teeth as she extended her arm.

Gently, he tugged back the sleeves of her windbreaker and sweatshirt then let out a soft hum. "I don't see any bones poking up under the skin. From the swelling and the start of some beautiful bruising, my money's on a sprain or a strain or maybe both."

Janice's lips drooped. "Kind of what I thought."

"I could be wrong, but either way, we need to get you to the hospital. You might need a stitch or two in that head wound also."

"Could you drive?" Every molecule of her independent streak protested the request, but what choice did she have?

"Happy to do it. Can you stand up?"

Janice nodded. Shane took her right elbow and helped support her weight as she struggled to her feet. A lifeline for a drowning person could scarcely have felt more welcome than his solid presence.

"Dizzy?" he asked.

"A little. My car is parked around the corner of the cottage. Here are the keys." Grimacing, she fished in her jeans' pocket and handed the ring to her rescuer.

"Let's go," he said. "But no faster than you're able."

Mild shivers coursed through Janice as Shane settled her into the passenger seat of the compact Ford. She reached for her seat belt, but he took the clip from her and leaned inside to snap the buckle into place. As his clean-cut profile paused near her face, a faint scent of lime and bay rum wafted to her nostrils.

Good taste in aftershave made another tick in the positive column for this new acquaintance. Janice closed her eyes as he withdrew and shut the car door. Too bad "acquaintance" was the most she could allow. She meant to keep her distance from anything and everything about this place. Completing her project here would sever the last link to her soiled family heritage.

The rear driver's-side door opened and soft snuffles announced Atlas jumping onto the seat. Then, of all things, the slide and click of the seat belt informed Janice that Shane had buckled in the dog. She glanced over her shoulder and solemn canine eyes met her gaze. The animal perched on his haunches, shoulder belt across his broad chest. The whiskery muzzle pulled back in a silent grin as if to say, "What's the matter, lady? Haven't you seen a dog in a seat belt before?"

A chuckle spurted between her lips, but a throb in her head cut the sound short. She pressed the heel of her right hand against her forehead then gingerly investigated the lump forming on the crown of her skull. Her fingertips encountered a sticky substance that was likely drying blood.

"Don't feel the area," Shane said as he slid into the driver's seat. "Germs."

"Right." Janice dropped her hand to her lap, eyeing the reddish residue on her fingers.

She must be a sight to behold. Beyond bedraggled, but why should she care? Even if this guy *was* cute and kind and smelled nice, she'd be gone in a few months, never to return.

Shane backed the car away from the cottage and another wave of dizziness swirled through her. As he headed the vehicle onto the dirt track that led toward the highway, Janice fought the urge to close her eyes again. If she didn't strive to stay oriented, the dizziness could easily lead to an embarrassing upheaval from her churning stomach.

"The nearest hospital is twenty miles away," Shane said:

"In Oak Bluffs. I checked such things out on the internet before I came to the island. With my refurbishing plans for the property, I wanted to be prepared for the off chance of an accident requiring medical attention. But I didn't figure on needing the services of a doctor quite so soon. I'd hoped not at all."

Shane gave her a sidelong look as they joined the sparse traffic on the paved highway. He opened his mouth as if to say something then closed it and returned his attention to the road.

"Good thing it's early in the season," he said at last. "When the tourists start mobbing the place, getting anywhere can be miserable. And forget about getting there fast. That's why a lot of folks rent bicycles."

"I may do that myself later on… Well, at least I was going to." She scowled at her injured arm. "Now a lot of things will have to wait until I'm fit again."

"You're going to continue with your plans for the cottage, ma'am?"

"It's Janice, not ma'am." She was in too much pain to conceal her annoyance at his terminology. You'd think she was in her dotage rather than no older than he was. Probably younger, in fact.

He let out a mellow laugh. The pleasant sound smoothed her hackles marginally.

"Sorry, Janice. In my EMT training, 'ma'am' is standard address for an adult female."

"You're an Emergency Medical Technician? I should have guessed from the way you handled things back at the cottage."

"Paramedic, actually, but I'm not practicing as such on-island."

"You're not from here? Of course not. You speak too crisply for a New Englander."

His shoulders rose and fell in a slow shrug. "And your lovely drawl drips Southern honey, not sea salt."

Janice clamped her lips closed. They'd established that neither of them was an island native, and both were here prior to the regular tourist season, so they weren't on vacation. His familiarity with traffic conditions during tourist season said he'd been here before, but the same could be said of lots of people. Like Shane, Janice had no intention of going into her history. Not that her curiosity wasn't piqued by this enigmatic stranger, but she could respect personal space.

Yeah, right, as her honorary niece Caroline would say. This tap and slide of verbal rapiers had energized her, chasing pain to the edges of her mind. A small grin tilted her lips. Getting to the bottom of Mr. Shane Gillum might be a pleasant distraction while she healed.

"Since I'll be out of commission for a while do you have any suggestions for how to go about hiring someone to handle the renovations?"

He pursed his lips and tilted this head. "You'll have to let me think about that one."

"Fair enough. Maybe someone at the hospital will have a lead for me. What brought you to my beach in the nick of time?"

"Our daily walk." Smiling, Shane jerked a thumb toward his dog, who offered a woof of confirmation.

"You live nearby?"

"Renting a ramshackle cabin about a quarter mile up the beach. I'll be here for the summer. Bumming, basically. Mulling over my future."

Had he experienced a recent trauma in his life, necessitating a change of direction? A divorce perhaps? His ring finger was as bare as hers. Or maybe his summer of discontent was due to boredom—though a career as a paramedic didn't sound too dull. Suffering from burnout more likely. She could be brassy from time to time, but she wasn't rude enough to ask the question outright.

"I might take up antiquing during my stay on the island," he went on. "I've heard Martha's Vineyard is a good place to pursue that hobby. Since you're embarking on cottage renovations, I assume you own the place." He shot her a raised-brow glance.

"I'm a Realtor and home stager by trade. The heir to the cottage has never lived anywhere near here and doesn't care to do so. The cottage hasn't been inhabited for nearly twenty years, so it's my task to supervise the process of getting it ready to sell."

There. She'd delivered the stock explanation she'd practiced in her mind on the flight to the island, and she'd even sounded casual about it. The words offered facts in a plausible light without betraying the whole truth that was none of anybody's business.

"Must be an interesting career." The frown in his voice negated his words.

She laughed then winced at a jab of pain in her head. "You don't sound too enthused."

Color tinted his cheeks. "No, I didn't mean… Well, what I meant was that it's probably fun, creative work, but it's got to be a hassle sometimes, pleasing your clients."

"What do you know? Somebody got the downside of my business in two seconds flat. Contrary clients. You're a perceptive man." She grinned. Now she was really starting to be sorry she couldn't be totally forthcoming with a guy this savvy and sympathetic.

He answered her smile. "I don't think that jolt on the noggin is going to have any lasting effect. You're pretty sharp yourself. I suppose when the work's done the owner will have to stop in and approve the work."

"Believe me the heir wants less than nothing to do with

the place. I have carte blanche, within a budget. The only ones I need to please are me and the buyer."

"Kind of a dream job then."

"So it would seem."

Janice pressed her lips together. This was supposed to be a simple in-and-out job, requiring a brief investment of time doing work she enjoyed. She hadn't counted on the complication of accidents, arranged or otherwise. It would be so nice to decide that the series of goofy mishaps was nothing more sinister than the result of a house in a state of disrepair. If not for the person standing on the porch when she'd emerged from the basement, she would probably be ready to stick to that conclusion. Now, questions reigned.

What should she make of the possibly malevolent trespasser? In her mind, the incident was eerie, but it could have simply been a curious local teenager—the figure had been too tall for a child. Or it might even have been an adult passerby. Grown-ups could be nosey, too. Then how did her mystery visitor disappear so quickly?

"Now you're the one who sounds less than enthusiastic."

Janice glanced at her impromptu chauffeur. His sober gaze and knotted brows questioned her, as if he sensed her troubled thoughts. She forced a thin smile. Unless she wanted to invite unwelcome inquiries, her fears and misgivings must remain her own for now.

"The whole picture changed when I messed myself up. There was a lot of work I wanted to do myself, now I— Look out!"

At a highway intersection, a midnight-blue SUV ignored a red light and roared toward her side of the lightweight car. Shane's plunge on the accelerator plastered Janice to her seat. Face shrouded under the bill of a wide-brimmed hat, the driver of the other vehicle laid on his horn. The blast rang in Janice's ears as the little Ford whizzed beyond the

SUV's massive bumper. The airstream of the near miss rocked the smaller vehicle.

From the backseat, Atlas let out a high-pitched whine.

"It's okay, buddy," Shane assured the animal.

Sucking a quavering breath into her lungs, Janice stared at his sober profile. Shane's Adam's apple bobbed as he kept his gaze locked on the road.

"Did you notice a license plate number?" he asked.

"Not hardly! I was too scared, and it happened so fast."

Her whole scalp prickled and her heart continued to bunny hop around her chest cavity as she stared warily out the window at passing traffic. This was too weird. Was the whole island warning her away? She'd left the family name and all such associations behind long ago, but did someone with a vendetta against the Morans know who she was? Unfortunately the number of people with reason to hate the Morans—any Moran—was legion. Or maybe she was just being paranoid.

"Traffic doesn't usually get so crazy this early in the season."

Shane's words drew her attention and she turned toward him. The droop of his lips and narrowed eyes betrayed troubled thoughts. Much like hers—only he couldn't know being with her might carry risk. Should she tell him?

No, she'd sound nuts, and she could be totally off base anyway. Maybe she was just having the proverbial bad day. Besides, if she explained her misgivings she'd have to expose who she was, and that was out of the question when her greatest desire was to bury her Moran legacy with depth and finality. Unless, of course, she was misreading the matter. If these accidents weren't accidents, and they weren't related to her family name, was the folly of her misspent youth coming home to roost—again? But events just prior to her retreat to Martha's Vineyard should have put an end to those consequences. The serial killer was dead and that was the end of the matter. Right?

Janice cast around in her mind for a change of direction in this conversation and a question occurred to her. "That's the second time you've mentioned knowledge about the tourist season. How often have you been here?"

"When I was a kid, we came to the island for a few weeks every July. Haven't been back since I was around twelve when my folks started preferring Florida, California or Mexico for our vacations."

"I see. You picked a 'mulling' spot that held pleasant memories."

He angled a one-sided grin toward her. "Discerning woman."

"No, that's my psychologist neighbor back in Denver."

"Denver? You can't have grown up there, either."

Janice forced a smile. It was a little late for biting her tongue. She'd revealed a tidbit of personal information, but then, so had he with that remark about his childhood vacations. What could it hurt to tell him where she'd grown up? Refusing to do so might seem suspicious.

"I was born and raised in Wilmington, South Carolina, but I haven't been back there since I lost my parents during my first year in college."

Silence fell for several blinks of Shane's eyes. "Sorry to hear about your loss," he finally said in strained tones.

"Me, too."

Janice clamped her lips shut. No one needed to know the details of the "loss" that still stung her heart like a thousand hornets. Maybe when she unloaded the last morsel of Moran property, she could heal and get on with her life... if dealing with the dilapidated condition of the cottage or negotiating island traffic didn't kill her first.

To save her sanity, she was going to believe recent events were unfortunate accidents. To save her life, she was going to keep her eyes peeled and senses sharp in case they weren't.

* * *

Seated in the waiting area of the emergency department at the Oak Bluffs hospital, Shane scowled at the blank wall opposite him. Other people's conversations droned in one ear and out the other. That was no accidental near-miss with the SUV on the way here. The driver had accelerated toward them, intending to ram them, or perhaps he'd meant to miss them but send a message. Was the message intended for him or for Janice?

He had come to Martha's Vineyard believing that none of the other Morans were aware of Reggie Moran's secret stop-off at his island property shortly before his fatal plane crash. Shane had also heard that the heir to the place was a fairly distant relative who didn't number on the crime family roster. Not that such a detail made the heir an upstanding citizen, but at least the person was not directly linked to the group that hunted Shane. However, even though the mob Morans might not be aware of Reggie's full itinerary on the day he died, they might be bent on shaking down any and every locality connected to Reggie, even a place that he hadn't, to their knowledge, visited for two decades.

How did Janice fit into the picture? The woman hadn't exactly been frank about the identity of the mystery heir or her relationship to the person. Was Janice hired through friendship with the Moran heir, or was she contracted as the result of someone who knew someone, which would indicate nothing more than an arm's length acquaintance? Either scenario was common enough, but whichever was the truth might tell him a lot about what sort of person Janice was. He'd yet to meet a Moran who wasn't as crooked as a dog's hind leg, and that went for their associates, too.

Had the saboteur seen through Shane's disguise, thus making them both targets? Maybe not. The SUV had aimed for the side where Janice was sitting, and she was the one with the injured wrist and bonk on the head. He needed to find a way to get a gander at that cellar step she said gave way beneath her. If that incident was pure chance he'd eat his socks.

Neither setup with the roof or the stairs guaranteed a fatal result but would easily cause injury, just as it had done, as well as discourage someone from pursuing renovation plans for the cottage. A spooked heir might let the place go for pennies on the dollar, say, to someone needing free rein and plenty of time to ransack the property. If Shane didn't know he wasn't the saboteur that criteria could apply to him.

The high stakes made the battle lines fierce between the Morans and him, but if his enemies were behind the sabotage and knew Janice was only an agent, not the actual owner of the property, the arranged accident scenario made a little more sense. Shane might even encourage himself to believe his cover had not been blown. In fact, it was more essential than ever that he remain undercover. If the wrong people recognized him as Seth Grange, his presence in Janice's vicinity would escalate the subtle hazing she was now experiencing into a death sentence in a hurry.

However, the forces who wanted the property left vacant wouldn't take kindly to Shane Gillum's interference on the agent's behalf, either. Maybe Shane would face a few of those arranged accidents himself, but watching out for those was better than the bullet to the brain he'd get if the Morans pierced his cover.

The cottage was not the only place that called for a thorough shakedown. His mention of antiquing had been deliberate. Maybe Janice would let him sort through the storage unit's contents in search of valuable items. She didn't need to know that the item of the greatest value would be the most current, and finding it was the best way to move her clear of danger. With God's help, maybe he could bring this terrible chapter in his life to a close without anyone else getting hurt—or at least any more hurt than she already was.

Shane consulted his watch. He needed to check on Atlas. It had been nearly an hour since Janice had disappeared into the bowels of the hospital for treatment, and Shane had left the dog in the car with a pair of the windows cracked open. Good thing the weather was cool. In a few weeks, temperatures were likely to shoot up significantly.

He rose and approached the small vending machine available to the people in the waiting area. A few coins sown into the machine reaped a bottle of water. The wastebasket next to the machine contained an empty cup that would meet canine needs.

Out in the parking lot, Atlas was sprawled in the backseat, panting lightly, tongue lolling. He seemed grateful for the water and said so with a few laps of the tongue on the hand that offered the refreshment. The dog's big, dusky eyes smiled at Shane, and he smiled back.

Amazingly his pulse didn't so much as skip a beat in handling this furry new friend. Shane might even keep the lovable galoot if he survived to succeed at his mission. Not that his knees wouldn't knock and his tongue cement to the roof of his mouth if any other large dog came within ten feet of him. He wasn't *that* phobia-free.

A grim smile spread Shane's lips. Only people with similar phobias could appreciate the emotional sweat equity he had put into making friends with Atlas. Wisely, he'd chosen a breed that, though large, was also particularly friendly. Atlas didn't seem to have an aggressive bone in his body, which made him a horrible guard dog but perfect as an identity-camouflaging companion for a guy with dog issues.

After taking Atlas on a brief walk to give him an opportunity to water a light pole, Shane returned the dog to the car and headed back into the hospital. From the hallway leading into the exam rooms, a willowy figure moved gracefully toward him, left arm in a navy blue sling.

Janice smiled when she saw him, dark eyebrows lifting toward a tousled wealth of chestnut-colored hair. He should have known straight off the bat that this was no Moran. He had yet to meet one—male or female—who didn't sport flaming hair and ruddy brows and lashes to match. Of course, her eyes *were* green like the Morans', and hair color could be changed—he should know—but dying the facial hair might be excessive. Most conclusive of all, this woman didn't *act* like any Moran he'd ever met.

"Hey," she said, halting in front of him, those green eyes frank and open. "Thanks for waiting. You didn't need to feel obligated to do that."

"I didn't feel obligated at all. Glad I could be here when you needed a hand. But I guess you're kind of stuck letting me use your car to drive back out to my place. I can drop you off wherever you're staying and then get another neighbor to follow me in my Jeep while I return your vehicle."

Her gaze went solemn. "That seems like an awful lot of bother. Glad I don't have to put you to it. I'm staying at the cottage, which is apparently right next to your place. I think I can handle letting you drop yourself off then taking the wheel the rest of the way home."

"You're joking, right? The place is falling apart around you, and you're going to sleep there? What about a bed… chairs…a table…food? Of course, you can always eat out in Chilmark or Menemsha. In fact, I can recommend any number of the seafood places, but—"

Janice cut him off with a wave of the hand and a laugh. "I appreciate your concern, Shane, but you should see the trunk of the car. It's stuffed with more than luggage. After I flew in this morning, I spent a few hours in Edgartown picking up anything I thought I might need to rough it for a few days. Besides, the electricity should be on by the time we return, and a guy is coming tomorrow to check out the pipes and the water heater before getting the water service restored. I'll be fine."

Shane puffed out a long breath and scratched his head. "You don't exactly strike me as the 'roughing it' type."

"Oh, really! What type do I strike you as?" Her tone teased, but her eyes narrowed.

Shane scrambled for the right words. He'd better not blow this deal now! He cleared his throat. "Would you think badly of me if I say 'soft dinner music and caviar on toast points'?"

"You'd put me in with the snooty set?"

"No, I was picturing more the grace and elegance set."

"Hmm." She tapped her lower lip, but a smile peeked out. "I'll accept that."

"Whew!" Shane passed a mock wipe across his forehead with the back of his hand, and she laughed.

"Does the doc say you're free to go?" he asked.

Janice lifted the sling-clad arm a few inches. "A hairline crack in a wrist bone, along with a bad sprain, as you thought. They gave me a short cast. And no stitches in my head, just a butterfly dressing. My brain seems sufficiently un-addled to require an observation stay in the hospital, so yes, I'm ready to blow this Popsicle stand."

Her bright gaze, brimming with wry humor, shot sparks of interest through him. He quenched them quickly.

"What did they give you for pain meds? Maybe you shouldn't drive at all."

"Nothing stronger than extra-strength ibuprofen."

"Still, it wouldn't hurt to spend a night at a comfy hotel or B and B in Oak Bluffs. I could come get you in the morning."

Please let her agree to a night away from the cottage.

He needed a chance to scout the place—check for signs of intruders, even use his amateur lock-picking skills to enter the premises and do whatever he could to make sure no more unpleasant surprises awaited the unsuspecting occupant. Who knew? He might even find what he was looking for and put an end to the threat altogether. It was the least he could do for someone thrust into a dangerous situation not of her own making.

But Janice shook her head. "I'm stubborn to a fault. That place is not going to get the best of me. I have a job to do, and I mean to see it through."

Shane studied the lifted chin and determined gaze of the woman before him. She meant what she said. In that case, it behooved him to stick to her as closely as possible, not only in hope of discovering what he needed to find, but to offer what protection he could.

"Are you still looking for someone to take over the non-professional tasks for you?"

Her eyes glinted like emeralds. "You know someone?"

Shane spread his arms. "You're looking at him."

He gazed into her wide eyes. What if she said no? His heart throbbed in his chest. How would he keep tabs on the situation? But what if she said yes? How would he keep himself objective and detached when the smiles this woman sent his way dizzied him like a knock on the noggin?

THREE

Janice's eyes popped open to find hazy fingers of dawn plucking at the edges of yellowed shades. Fat chance she'd get any more sleep. She'd struggled for the few hours she'd obtained. The hazardous events of yesterday haunted her.

What should she make of all the crazy things that had happened? True accidents or arranged? Was someone out to get her, or was she just skittish from her recent brush with death in Denver or because of the taint of her birth family? How could she know the difference? Probably not by running away, though the option appealed like a high, dry cave in a monsoon. She couldn't live life huddled in the dark behind stone walls. Whatever was going on, she had to face it. Maybe yesterday was a fluke and today would be smooth sailing. No way to find out until she got up and plunged into the tasks ahead.

Janice gathered her muscles to sit up but subsided with a huff onto her inflated mattress. Her battered body objected to a perky start. Scowling, she looked around her Spartan surroundings in the larger of the cottage's two bedrooms. The only adornments were gossamer cobwebs dangling from the ceiling. The few utilitarian objects scattered about had come inside with her.

Her suitcase yawned open in one corner. A lamp she'd bought in Edgartown sat on the floor in the opposite corner. Nothing decorated the weathered walls, not so much as a mirror, which she no doubt badly needed. She ran her tongue over her teeth. A toothbrush would be welcome, also.

There was a silvered mirror in the dilapidated bathroom, a toothbrush in her suitcase and jugs of water in the kitchen to take care of her liquid ablutions until the water was restored whenever the plumber came today. Provided the plumbing still worked after all this time, she'd be able to take a shower. Until then, she would have to be downright eighteenth century in caring for her personal needs.

The notion had been in the category of minor inconvenience until her accidents of yesterday. Now the simplest activities could be a challenge, but she'd manage. She had to. Staying at a public place and answering well-meant questions from strangers was out of the question when she'd come here for privacy and anonymity.

Finally, steeling herself against the aches and pains, Janice eased upright and gingerly stretched—with one arm anyway—then stuffed her feet into a pair of mule slippers. Yawning, she shuffled to the kitchen where her food, toaster, hot plate and cleaning supplies waited.

Yesterday when she and Shane returned from the hospital, the electricity was on—thankfully. And thank goodness for electric baseboard heat. At least the cottage was nicely warm this morning. Janice had a haunting reason to dread a cold environment. Not something she was going to allow herself to think about this morning. She pushed away the memory as she reached for a fresh bottle of water from the vintage 1950s refrigerator that went nicely with the scuffed and chipped burnt-orange countertops.

Shane had given up on urging her to seek out the comfort of a hotel and insisted on carrying everything from her trunk into the cottage. He'd made several trips to the tune of her warning about that faulty porch board. He'd even blown up her mattress with the help of the electronic air pump, calling the gadget "pretty slick," then helped unpack and put away all her kitchen items.

"You've got enough here to see you through a brief famine." He'd laughed as he stowed boxes and cans. He had a nice laugh.

Bathed in early morning sunrays that reached her through the kitchen window, Janice's spirits took an upturn. Her unexpected helper was turning out to be equal parts amusing and exasperating. Shane had been a total mother hen about leaving her here alone last night, but she'd been firm, and at last he'd taken Atlas and headed out with a final admonishment to get a landline phone installed ASAP.

Yes, Sergeant Gillum, she'd thought and nearly saluted. After what they'd been through, he'd probably felt as though he had a stake in her well-being. What would she have done without him? Matters would probably have gone quite differently yesterday without his help.

Janice sobered. Was Shane Gillum among God's ways of assisting her through this rough patch or were things coming together too easily? Not that her injuries equated to easy, but her replacement worker had popped up effortlessly, seemingly out of nowhere. Should she be suspicious?

Suspicion and paranoia were family traits—the guilty were naturally suspicious of others. Since she had no guilty reasons for coming here to dispose of this property, she'd like to choose a different reaction. Shane had showed up when she'd needed someone and then gone above and beyond to be helpful.

He appeared to be a private sort, as she was herself. In all other respects, he'd proved compassionate and helpful. Just a guy looking for some peace of mind through a change of scenery. Again, they had a lot in common.

Hopefully, they would work together well—he'd work and she'd supervise, that is.

If he was starting a new antiquing hobby, she'd been told the storage unit in Edgartown held quite a few pieces. She'd yet to check out the contents and would need help when she started sorting through things. Shane would come in more than handy. Some items she might use to stage the cottage for sale. Others she could sell outright. Maybe Shane would be interested in some of the pieces in exchange for his work. Then her budget wouldn't be so strained. Who knew? Maybe she'd find a few things to keep for herself.

What was she thinking? Janice shook her head as she capped the bottle of water. She wanted nothing that bore the Moran stain. Whatever she couldn't sell or exchange for labor would go into the nearest trash bin.

An hour later she'd washed, dressed with a bit of an awkward struggle in a sweatshirt and jeans, and brushed her teeth and hair. After numerous one-handed attempts, she'd finally managed to gather her heavy locks away from her face and into a loose ponytail bound with a large hair clip.

Tired before the day had any traction under it she leaned against the kitchen counter while her bagel toasted. Her breakfast popped up just as the porch boards squealed and a knock sounded on the door. Glancing from the steaming, golden-brown goodness to the front door and back again, she sighed and headed to answer the knock. If Shane's early-bird habits were going to cause her a cold meal, she'd dock his pay. Well, at least she'd razz him a little.

Janice opened the door, a quip on her tongue, but the words froze behind her teeth. The most unusual person she'd ever seen in her life—and she'd seen a few—gazed at her with bright hazel eyes rimmed in a virtual rainbow of eye shadow. The woman was about a head and a half shorter than Janice but nearly as wide as the doorway. She wore a floral print, muumuu-style dress under a crisp white apron edged in eyelet lace. A knitted shawl hugged sturdy shoulders, and a silver-white, beehive hairdo rose to a height that a more slender neck might find difficult to support. She hugged a small paper sack to her ample bosom.

"Hi, there," the woman said with a beaming smile framed in vivid red lipstick. The word *there* came out "they-ah." Definitely a native New Englander.

"Hello." Janice tried a return smile, but it probably didn't succeed as much more than a puzzled grimace.

"When I heard someone was out at the old Moran place, I could scarcely believe my ears. But here you are, pretty as a picture." The woman bobbed her several chins.

"I take it the rumor mill is alive and well on Martha's Vineyard." So much for a low profile.

"You got that right, lambkin, and second to none." The woman grinned and rocked on pudgy feet overflowing serviceable brown clogs. "I apologize that it's taken a while for me to find a spare minute to drop by. I knew someone was here a couple of days ago when some fishermen at sea reported spotting lights up at the old Moran place. Scared their hair frizzy. They were talkin' all crazy-like about ghosts and long-dead pirates, but I told 'em in no uncertain terms to stow their imaginations. There's always a sensible explanation, and I'm lookin' at her. I—"

"That's impossible." Janice burst into the woman's chatter.

"What's impossible?" The rainbow eyes blinked at her.

"Lights. Here. Days ago. I didn't arrive on the island until yesterday morning, and the electricity wasn't turned on until yesterday afternoon."

"Well, what do you know about that?" Her guest frowned. "I'm thinkin' some jackdaws bored of a poor night's fishin' got a snoot full and started tellin' each other stories about bootleggers and pirates. Imagined the lights out of the reflection of the moon on the water."

Janice inhaled a deep breath. Pirates? Bootleggers? Typical activities of her ancestors. But no peg-legged, eye-patched ghost was behind the strange clump of accidents she'd encountered since reaching Martha's Vineyard. If those things were sabotage, they'd been carried out by flesh and blood.

"Sorry to see you've met with difficulties." Her guest nodded toward Janice's sling. "Please tell me you didn't get hurt on our island."

"I can't assure you of that, but it was my own fault for not watching my step going down into the basement." For now, Janice would count that version true, unless examination of the broken step told a different story.

The woman clucked. "I was on my way to work this morning and just had to see if I'd heard right. Then I saw your lights were on for real, so I thought I'd stop and introduce myself. Esther Mae Furbish here. Essie Mae to my friends, and that's everyone!" She burbled a laugh that drew a genuine smile from Janice.

"I'm Janice Swenson, the Realtor handling renovation and sale of the property."

"Sale, you say? Place like this'll bring a pretty nickel with all those off-islanders hungry for vacation homes." Essie Mae's lips pursed as though she'd sucked something sour, but then she broke into her infectious grin. "Guess I should be grateful for the summer swarms. Without the tourist trade my job would be in jeopardy. My little place is next one up the road from here, Chilmark-way. You couldn't buy it off me for love or money. To hang on to it, I wait tables at the Beach Shanty in Menemsha. You stop on in someday soon for the best chowder on the island. If

I'm not there, tell 'em Essie Mae sent you, and you'll get a 10 percent discount."

"Thank you. I appreciate the offer." A stiff breeze whooshed across the porch, ruffling the fringe on Essie Mae's shawl and lapping at Janice with a chilly tongue. She shivered.

"Here I am keeping you standing in the doorway with my jawing." Essie Mae hugged her shawl close, displaying glittery blue nail polish and an eclectic array of rings on every finger, including the thumb.

"Would you like to come in?" Janice stood back.

Maybe she could share her bagel or even toast another one, but she'd be challenged to know where to seat a guest with only a folding camp chair available. Apparently she needed to remedy the furniture situation sooner rather than later if curious neighbors were going to be stopping by.

"Another time, lambkin. Like I said, I'm due at work." Essie Mae checked her watch and let out a little squeak. "Better scoot. Here you are." She extended the brown paper bag. "Mulberry preserves. Made 'em myself."

"Thank you." Janice took the bag. "I don't know what to say."

"You already said it, lambkin. Thank you is more than enough." She waggled be-ringed fingers, turned and took a step away from the door. "Whoops!" Her arms flapped as she regained her balance. "Soft spot in the floorboards, dear," she said over her shoulder. "Good luck to you. The place needs a lot of TLC."

"So sorry about that," Janice called as Essie Mae hustled off the porch, holding her towering hairdo in place against the wind.

Janice's pulse fluttered in her throat. She'd forgotten about the treacherous footing until it was too late to warn her guest. Unless she wanted to be liable for someone's broken leg, she'd better address the porch boards first thing.

She returned to the kitchen, shaking her head. A smile tugged at the corners of her lips as she pulled the jar of preserves from the bag. Her mouth watered. What a thoughtful woman. And entertaining, too! If circumstances were different, Janice might enjoy a stay on the island.

At least now she had something yummier than margarine to spread on her bagel. A few more seconds in the toaster would warm it again. She pressed the toaster lever down as the creaky porch announced another visitor or maybe the return of the same.

With a groan, Janice headed for the door. A knock sounded, punctuated by a loud crack and a canine yelp. Atlas! She broke into a run.

At the sound of splintering wood and a high-pitched yip, Shane whirled from the door and dropped his gaze to find Atlas struggling to free his right hind leg that was buried in a hole in the floorboards. Scolding himself for allowing the dog to frisk around the rickety porch while he knocked, Shane knelt and placed his hand on the whimpering animal's head.

"Steady there, boy." The gentle words and touch must have ministered some comfort because Atlas stopped trying to tug his leg from between the boards and subsided, panting, onto the porch.

"Oh, no!" Janice knelt by his side.

"Pet him and calm him while I work his leg out," Shane said.

She immediately complied, cooing to the animal and stroking his head. Atlas's eyes rolled up in doggy bliss and he relaxed further.

"Perfect." Shane gave Janice a grateful look.

Faint shadows under her eyes betrayed a fitful night's

sleep, but other than that he'd rarely seen a more attractive female completely devoid of makeup. The crisp temperature nipped color into her cheeks and her emerald gaze glowed in the sun's early rays.

Jerking his attention from her riveting face, Shane worked his hands down between Atlas's haunch and the boards. A few slivers pricked the skin of his hands and the backs of his wrists, but he paid no attention as he worked the dog's furry leg upward in gentle pulls.

At last the animal sprang free and jumped up, knocking Janice over. She let out a soft squawk as she landed on her back. Atlas took her position as an invitation to bathe her face with his tongue. Laughter vied with spluttering as she received the dog's adoration.

Shane grabbed Atlas's collar with a stern command to sit. The dog obeyed, but gazed up at him with innocent surprise written on his whiskery face. Shane suppressed a smile. He couldn't have his pet bowling people over and nearly drowning them in slobber, particularly someone who was already injured.

He knelt beside Janice, who was struggling one-handed into a sitting position. "Are you all right?"

"Just fine." She wiped her face with the sleeve of her sweatshirt. "Guess I've had my bath this morning, though. How's Atlas?"

"He's good. I think his fur cushioned him from scrapes or slivers, which is more than I can say for myself." He grimaced at bits of wood sticking from his skin and small amounts of blood welling from a few raw scrapes.

"Come inside," Janice said. "There's a first-aid kit among all that stuff you unloaded for me yesterday."

Letting out tiny groans, she began to rise. Shane reached out to help her, but she batted him away with a chuckle.

"I may be bruised and battered, but I'll manage to stand on my own two feet, thank you. But now you've got war wounds, and we haven't even begun to fight the restoration battle."

She led the way to the door and shoved it open. Smoke billowed out, along with the unmistakable reek of burned bread.

"My bagel!" she cried.

Shane burst out laughing. He couldn't help himself. Her expression was so comical, as if her greatest treasure had been ruined. She shot him a scowl and then her lips broke apart in a grin.

She shook her head. "Are you as good a fireman as you are a paramedic? We need to open some windows and clear the smoke out of here. Then I'll play EMT on those scrapes and slivers."

"After that we go buy lumber to fix that break on the porch."

"Great minds," she quipped, eyes twinkling.

Shane's pulse did a funky little jig and he quickly turned away and got busy prying windows open. A few minutes later he sat in the folding camp chair, while Janice knelt beside him picking slivers out of his skin with tweezers. A scent of smoke lingered in the air and Atlas went about sniffing every corner, nook and cranny. Shane fisted the hand she wasn't working on. What got into him that he barely restrained the impulse to reach out and touch the wealth of shimmering chestnut hair that masked her face?

This tender, compassionate woman was no Moran. She probably hadn't a clue what sort of crime family her employer came from…or what danger the jerk had sent her into. If Shane thought it would keep this innocent Realtor safe, he'd be tempted to go away. Right now, the best thing Janice had going for her as long as she refused to leave the island was his watchful presence.

"How about I try again with the bagels?" she asked as she finished cleaning and dressing the minor wounds.

"Better yet, how about I treat us to breakfast this morning? The nearest lumberyard is Vineyard Haven. I know because I bought a few things there last week. It's only a hop and a skip out of our way to stop at this great home-cooking place in Menemsha."

Janice lifted her eyebrows. "Let me guess: The Beach Shanty."

"You're kidding me." Shane laughed. "Essie Mae's been by here already?"

"She visited you, too?"

"Day after my arrival on the island. I think she fancies herself a one-woman Welcome Wagon."

"Either that or she gets a commission for every bowl of chowder she sells."

"That chowder would sell itself. My mouth is watering already."

"Chowder for breakfast?"

"Don't knock it until you try it."

"With a challenge like that, I guess it'll be two bowls of chowder. Essie Mae will be thrilled. What a unique character. I think I like her."

"Me, too."

Essie Mae was the sort of affable soul people took to right away. Janice was deep and sometimes hard to read, but already he liked her more than he had bargained for, and they'd been acquainted for only one day—granted under extreme circumstances that could create an atmosphere for rapid bonding.

This woman was hiding something, though. Something that troubled her deeply. What could it be? Was it just that she suspected her accidents weren't so accidental? Or was there more to her burden? Whatever the issue, they would have to talk about it. The problem with the discussion idea was that he had things to hide, also.

"Give me a little help with a tape measure," Shane said,

"and we'll jot down length, width and depth of the existing porch before we take off. Shouldn't hold us up but a few minutes."

Janice grabbed a pad of scratch paper and a pencil. She proved familiar with handling a tape measure in tandem with someone else. Probably came with the Realtor territory. As he knelt on the ground to take the height measurement, his knee pressed into the mellow earth next to the piece of the broken roof tile he'd been examining yesterday. His conscience smote him. She needed to be alerted even if he dared not offer her the reasons why.

Shane picked up the tile and handed it to her where she knelt on the edge of the porch. "Notice anything?"

She examined the edges of the tile and her lips pressed together with a soft humph. "It wasn't an accident, was it?" Her gaze met his. Did he detect a smidgeon of relief glowing in the green depths? "I was starting to wonder about all these strange things happening, but I didn't know how to say so without sounding paranoid or making excuses for clumsiness."

Shane nodded. So she'd been worried that he'd think she was seeing threat where none existed or that he'd interpret any protest as a cover-up for a fault. He could understand that motivation.

"Clumsy is not a word I associate with you," he said. "As for deliberate sabotage? At the very least, the marks look suspicious."

"Agreed, but whoever did this couldn't know the tile would come down on top of someone."

"But there was a decent chance of it. Particularly if anyone knew the place was about to be renovated, and there would be a good deal of traffic and probably hammering and bumping and thumping."

Janice frowned and her expression went distant. Then

her gaze met his, grim and solid. "I surprised an intruder on my porch yesterday—just before you showed up."

"Who was it?"

"No clue. Except he—or she—was shorter than you. Probably shorter than me, too. The person was peering through the picture window. All I could make out was the outline of a face and part of a torso. I felt like..." Her voice trailed off.

"What?"

"Nothing. Probably my imagination. You know, because I was so startled, I got the feeling the intruder meant me harm."

"And here you have the proof." Shane tapped the broken tile.

"No, if the trespasser had been sawing on the roof right before I caught him, I would have heard the noise."

"The person could have been here before, you know. Maybe the intruder came back to check on his or her handiwork."

Janice sat back on her haunches. "Could be. In fact, Essie Mae said some fishermen saw lights up here a few nights ago. But what would be the point of booby-trapping this place?"

Shane dropped his gaze to the tape measure. He couldn't answer that question—truthfully anyway. "Let's just be extra careful from now on, okay?"

"Should we report this to the police?"

Her voice inflection said that she dreaded that option almost as much as he did, but he wouldn't discourage the measure—not when her safety was involved. "Probably a good idea."

She sighed. "All right. Maybe there will be an office in Menemsha or Vineyard Haven where we can file a report. I just hate—" She bit her lip, her gaze on the rippling ocean. "I mean, I so wanted this job to go smoothly."

"Rumors of a saboteur could hurt a sale."

"True." She sent him a wry smile. "But from a few things Essie Mae let drop, this place already has an unsavory reputation. Some of the locals apparently consider it haunted."

Shane shrugged. "An air of mystery might have extra appeal to a certain sort of buyer."

"Way to cheer me up." She bopped him companionably on the shoulder. "We're burning daylight so we'd better get this last measurement and be on our way."

Soon they had all the figures they needed and headed for Shane's Jeep. He insisted on driving his vehicle. Janice countered by insisting on paying for gas. The debate ended in Shane's surrender on the gas issue as he buckled Atlas into the backseat.

"You're either a really good guy or a very bad driver," Janice said as Shane slipped into the driver's seat.

"What makes you say that?" He started the vehicle.

She laughed. "It takes an unusually conscientious pet owner to buckle his dog into a seat belt, or else a pet owner who has serious reservations about his driving ability."

Shane shook his head, grinning. "How about this option? I'm a nervous new pet owner who happened to adopt a dog that tolerates neurotic behavior in his master. I'm sure Atlas would rather stick his head out the window and let his tongue flap in the breeze."

"That explanation works, too."

The short trip passed in pleasant small talk and soon they drove into a tiny fishing village. A large statue of a marlin welcomed them to the community. Boats from dinghy-size to fishing trawlers to majestic schooners lined piers that stretched long fingers into the green-blue ocean. With the jumble of masts piercing the skyline, the land-cupped bay resembled a massive toothpick holder.

Shane brought the Jeep to a halt in a parking place

across the street from a clapboard structure with portholes for windows and colorful sea creatures painted in framed sections of the exterior. Over the red-painted door hung what looked like a hand-scrawled sign proclaiming The Beach Shanty.

His passenger let out a small giggle. "This place is as unique-looking as its waitress."

"I'd say they belong together. Actually, Essie Mae is part owner."

"Good for her," Janice said as she emerged from the vehicle.

"Wait here," Shane told Atlas as he unbuckled him. "I'll bring you a fresh-baked biscuit."

The dog whiffled softly and stretched out in the seat.

Shane turned in time to see Janice begin crossing the street. Traffic was sparse. The types of rugged vehicles chugging down the road suggested fishermen and other laborers going about their tasks. He began to follow Janice across, but the rev of an engine swiveled Shane's head toward the intersection behind them.

A large, rattletrap pickup squealed around the corner, Janice and Shane in the path of its rusty grille.

"Look out!" he shouted and raced toward her.

FOUR

An engine roar, the scream of skidding tires and a male shout melded into a bewildering cacophony as Janice gaped at an oncoming truck. She ordered her feet to move, but they'd clamped onto the pavement. A firm body barreled into her and she flew forward. Instinctively cradling her injured wrist, she landed hard on her left side. Air gushed from her lungs.

She tumbled across gritty pavement like a crazed rolling pin. The residue of gas fumes invaded her nostrils from the weathered asphalt. A curb abruptly halted her ungainly whirl even as a solid boom, the screech of crumpling metal and crunch of shattering glass reverberated in her ears.

Dazed, Janice stared up into a blue sky swirling with white wisps. Gradually the pinwheel stilled and the clouds settled into lazily drifting puffs of white. Heavy silence draped the atmosphere. She drew in a deep breath. Excited woofs from Atlas broke the illusion of calm as voices shouted and running feet converged from every direction.

Wincing at the sting of a skinned elbow, Janice inched gingerly up onto one palm. Less than fifty feet away on her side of the street sat the runaway pickup, hood crumpled around a light pole. A small crowd was forming at the scene. Their excited voices blurred into white noise in her ears. Suddenly a vivid-hued female face blocked her view—Essie Mae, wide-eyed and wringing her hands in her apron.

"Are you all right, lambkin? Such a thing! I never!" The rainbow-lined gaze shot sparks as she scowled over her shoulder at the pickup. "I've been tellin' that Bill Beaseley to get the brakes fixed on that rattletrap, but his fishin' trawler's about the only thing he'll spend a dime on. Now look what's happened."

"I-Is Mr. Beaseley okay? Oh, my…Shane!" Janice stared wildly around as she struggled to rise. "Was he hit?"

Essie Mac's pudgy hand pressed her down with a stern tut-tut. "Let's get you looked at by Amy Covington before you get too spry. Amy's a licensed practical nurse, and she's the closest thing to a doctor that Menemsha boasts."

"Essie, I appreciate your concern, but there's nothing wrong with me that a little disinfectant and a couple of adhesive strips can't patch up. I'm not going to lie here for who knows how long until some nurse is brought in. Shane's a paramedic. If he's okay, he can—"

"Take it easy, Tuff. I'm all right."

Shane's voice brought Janice's head up. He limped toward her, clutching an outer thigh where a rent showed in his jeans. No blood, though, and he walked without assistance. Something about his lopsided grin shot a thrill through her. What had he called her? Tuff? The warmth in his eyes made the term a compliment, though she begged to differ on the accuracy. She'd been scared stiff—literally. His quick reaction had saved them both.

Shane offered a hand. She took it and he tugged her to her feet. A mild wave of dizziness passed through her, but she shoved it away. Tough people didn't faint. They might get knocked for a loop by falling pieces of roof slate, but they didn't collapse from a mere brush with death.

"Did you go for a tumble, too?" She motioned toward the rip in his jeans.

"Top over tail. I think my britches tangled with that raggedy bumper and came out the loser."

"You could have been killed!"

"*We* could have been, but we weren't."

"Flat lucky is what I say." Essie Mae planted her fists on ample hips as she gazed up at Shane with narrowed eyes. "You're a paramedic? I didn't know that." Her tone conveyed mild affront that she'd been in the dark about such an important detail regarding a newcomer to her stomping grounds.

Janice suppressed a smile.

"Everyone okay?" a deep voice rasped. A short, stocky man in jeans and a long-sleeved, button-down shirt that had seen better days hustled toward them with a rolling gait, as if he walked a boat deck rather than solid street. "That was a wicked-close call. My brakes went out."

"Not surprising with that bucket of bolts you insist on drivin', Bill Beaseley." Essie Mae wagged a finger and scowled at the fisherman.

"Aw, now, Essie. I just had them brakes worked on, and they was fine, ayuh." He folded his arms across a thick chest. "Don't know why they give out now. I couldn't get her to stop or slow down, even though I was mashin' my foot on the brake pedal clean to the floorboards."

The knot between Janice's shoulder blades eased marginally. If the situation weren't so serious, the confrontation between these two feisty locals would be worth a chuckle.

"Why didn't you at least lay on the horn to let folks know you were out of control?" The color on Essie's jowls deepened from grapefruit to strawberry.

Bill shifted from one foot to another, gaze darting everywhere but on his tormenter. "Horn ain't worked for coupla years."

Essie Mae sniffed. "You drive too fast in the first place."

Bill scowled. "Well, the old girl is toast now, so that should make you happy." He lifted a sheepish gaze toward Janice and Shane. "I'm right sorry, folks."

"Are you all right?" Janice motioned toward one side of Bill's face that was speckled with bright red flecks.

"Aw, that." He rubbed his cheek against a flannel shirt sleeve, leaving pinkish streaks on the already stained fabric. "Windshield glass shattered. Musta peppahed me a bit."

"Well, come on then." Essie Mae motioned toward the restaurant. "If you're all ambulatin' and don't need an ambulance, you'd best step on in and have a bowl of chowder to calm your nerves. On the house."

"Me, too?" Bill piped in, gaze brightening.

"You, too, scalawag. Amy'll be here directly to apply a little first aid while Mitch takes your statements."

"Mitch is a police officer, I assume?" Shane's expression twisted as if he'd swallowed something distasteful and his gaze went shuttered.

Janice frowned and narrowed her eyes. Given Mr. Beaseley's history of neglecting vehicle maintenance, and his open remorse, as well as the loss of his pickup, it was hard to call this dust-up anything but a genuine accident. Reporting the matter to the authorities was a matter of course, so why would police involvement make Shane Gillum nervous?

Less than an hour ago Janice had sensed his reluctance to recommend reporting yesterday's incidents at the cottage to the authorities, but then, he couldn't very well counsel against the action without sounding guilty of something. Was he? After all, he'd been on the island before she'd arrived—long enough to do the damage to that roof. Plus if he'd been standing bent slightly at the knees or leaning forward to peer in, Shane could have been the mystery intruder at her window.

But there the logic trail dead ended. Shane couldn't possibly have reached the beach, much less have gotten himself and his dog out of sight for a later reappearance as the saving hero in the time it had taken her to rush out the door of the cottage in pursuit. Also, he was the one who had pointed out the tool marks on the roof tile. Furthermore, he had showed himself kind and helpful yesterday, and now brave and quick-witted in saving both their lives.

Yet those characteristics didn't eliminate the possibility that he had something to hide from the law. Something that didn't involve her. Was a legal problem his motive for retreating to Martha's Vineyard?

Then again, Shane could be one of those people who got uncomfortable dealing with cops. Lots of people felt that way. Janice gave a mental shake of the head. That idea didn't make sense. In his line of work, he must have gotten used to working closely with police personnel on EMT call-outs.

Maybe she was reading too much into a fleeting reaction in a stressful situation. Or maybe she had reason to be cautious around this man who had so quickly insinuated himself into her life.

"That was a close call! Thank you again for your quick action."

Janice's soft-voiced words from the booth seat across from Shane slathered guilt on top of the anxiety that soured his gut. If she knew who he really was and why he was sticking so close to her, she'd probably belt him, and he wouldn't blame her. Even if she wasn't a Moran and was innocent of any complicity in their crooked ways, he could never come clean with her now. She'd hate his guts and give him the boot. He couldn't risk being barred from the place he needed to search. Best if he finished his business on the Moran property, kept Janice safe the best he could, and then disappeared from her life forever.

Lord, how did doing the necessary thing turn so complicated?

A bustling waitress—not Essie Mae—plunked a steaming bowl of chowder in front of him. Rich odors of seafood and creamy stock filled his nostrils. His taste buds moistened even as his stomach clenched. He had to see this through. Just as he had to smile and eat this chowder, whether the acid churning in his empty belly welcomed the intrusion or not.

"Hey, we're alive." Janice's words were followed by a gentle touch on the back of his hand.

Shane mustered a tight smile. "I guess it's just registering with me how close we came to being roadkill. This incident has the earmarks of a genuine accident, but on top of everything else, it's just weird."

"I was thinking the same thing."

Shane pushed the steaming bowl away from him. "I don't know if I can eat this."

Janice leaned over her chowder and inhaled noisily. "Oddly enough, I'm ravenous and hot chowder sounds like the perfect balm for my ravaged nerves."

He gusted a laugh and rolled tension from his shoulders. "I'm sure Essie Mae would agree with your philosophy. And you don't need to thank me for saving you. I thank God for saving us both."

Shane liked to be nonconfrontational but open about his faith. In this case a little God-talk might help him sort out his thoughts about Janice if he knew where she stood with the Almighty.

"Me, too."

Her gaze lit as she smiled and a layer of Shane's defenses melted. Whether that was a good thing or not remained to be seen.

"Would you say grace?" she asked.

Shane bowed his head. He'd take her hand, but that felt a little too forward at this point, and probably not a good idea at any time, considering his need to remain objective and detached. As if keeping emotional distance wasn't already in serious jeopardy.

Bowing his head, he dragged his thoughts from the woman across from him and on to the One who kept them in the palm of His hand. Best remember Who was his most important ally. He concluded the brief prayer with a firm "Amen" and lifted his gaze to Janice's with a smile.

She smiled back and they hefted their spoons in unison.

Soft slurping and appreciative hums were briefly interrupted by the advent of an angular woman with stern eyes who dabbed antiseptic on Janice's skinned elbow and asked about the arm in a sling. When she heard that the injury had occurred yesterday and had already been examined by a doctor, she lost interest in Janice and turned toward Shane. He informed Amy Covington that his bruised leg required no first aid, and the nurse went off with a sniff to tend Mr. Beaseley's glass cuts.

"Are house calls—er, restaurant calls—usual on Martha's Vineyard?" Janice asked.

Shane shrugged, his gaze straying to the LPN bent over Bill Beaseley, dabbing at his face with a cotton ball. In the relative dimness of this dark-timbered building, it was difficult to read facial expressions from any distance, but body language conveyed a warmth of concern that had been lacking in the woman's approach to Janice and him.

"Islanders do things their own way. I suspect we were included in the personal attention because a native vouched for us."

"Essie Mae?"

"Probably. And Nurse Covington would want to do her

part to ensure a local fisherman doesn't get sued by a pair of greedy off-islanders."

"The residents rally to protect their own."

"Exactly. As a boy, I had a couple of local friends I hung out with when our family vacationed here. Those associations gave me the impression the entire island was like a giant Mayberry—if you lived here year-round."

"And if not?"

"You are a means to bread and butter, but they don't care to absorb any of your cosmopolitan ways."

Janice laughed. "Edgartown struck me as pretty up-to-date despite the deliberate quaintness of the shops."

"Times they do change."

"Not so much in Menemsha." Essie Mae gazed benignly down at them, one hand on an ample hip, the other cradling a wash rag. "How was the chowder?"

"Fabulous!"

"Wonderful!"

Their exclamations stumbled over each other and Essie Mae beamed. "Here comes Mitch just in time to catch you before you get on with the business of your day."

She motioned toward a bowling ball on stilts trundling toward them. Janice's gaze widened even as Shane lost the battle against his jaw dropping.

Essie Mae chuckled and leaned toward them. "Just between you and me, if that guy's middle gets any rounder and his legs any skinnier, he'll travel faster rolling than walking. But make no mistake," she said, stooping even closer, "he don't take no nonsense. Make short work of that Bill Beaseley, he will. You don't have to worry about that." She swiped at the table with the rag in her hand then turned on her heel and scuttled toward the kitchen.

Seconds later Officer Mitch stopped at their table and gazed down at them with owl eyes magnified behind telescopic-lens glasses. Shane's throat closed and he deposited his spoon in his nearly empty bowl. His expensive but fake ID hadn't been tested by the eyes of a cop.

"You'd be the tourists who walked out into traffic and nearly got hit?" the officer asked.

Janice's gaze, brimming with confusion, shifted to Shane.

He frowned up at the policeman. "I'm not sure how you came by that idea, but the facts don't match that statement."

"That so?" The officer rocked back on his heels and grinned, though the gray eyes remained sober—watchful. "Why don't you let me have the *facts,* then?"

"We parked opposite the restaurant. Janice got out of the vehicle and started across the street while I made sure my dog was all right. By the time I turned around, a pickup truck was careening around the corner and barreling straight for her."

Janice jumped in. "That's exactly what happened, Officer. We weren't exactly in a crosswalk, but no vehicles were coming when I started out. If Shane hadn't risked his own life to save mine, I'm pretty sure I wouldn't be talking to you right now."

Shane's face heated. She made him sound like a hero, when he actually hadn't given a second thought to what he was doing—just reacted.

"I don't think Mr. Beaseley meant to hit either of us," Janice rushed on. "He could have been hurt or killed, too, ramming into that light pole. I understand his pickup hasn't been running the best..." Her words trailed off with more of a question lilt than a statement.

Officer Mitch made a noncommittal noise in his throat. He pointed toward her. "You'd be Janice." He swiveled his finger. "And you'd be Shane. Got any ID?"

Jaw tensed, Shane dug his wallet out of his back pocket and produced his fabricated license. The plastic card had better be worth what he'd paid for it. He hadn't known it would feel so bad to try to fool the authorities. Was presenting a false ID illegal if he wasn't under suspicion for anything or up to illegal activities—just trying to save his own skin?

He wasn't about to ask. Even if Shane and the officer had been alone, he wouldn't have dared come clean. The Morans could easily have as much clout with the Martha's Vineyard police department as they did in departments all up and down the East Coast. Another reason he wasn't so sure reporting the sabotage to the authorities would produce any good results, but he could hardly explain that issue to Janice.

Somber-faced, she produced her driver's license from the fanny pack she'd donned before they'd left the cabin. Her mouth twisted into a lopsided frown and her drawn brows nearly met in the middle of her forehead. Why did she look so uncomfortable about proving her identity? Surely she was who she said she was. They couldn't both be hiding behind aliases. Could they?

Instead of looking at the driver's licenses, Officer Mitch eyed Janice's sling. "You injured enough to see a doctor?"

"Prior injury." Janice expelled an audible breath through her nose. "You won't have to put it in your report."

Shane raised his eyebrows at her. Why didn't she take this opportunity to mention the likely sabotage at the cottage? Janice caught his gaze with an infinitesimal shake of the head. Something must be giving her cold feet about reporting to the authorities. Maybe it was this guy's stone-cold demeanor.

The policeman studied their licenses. "Where are you staying on-island?"

Shane told him about his rental shack without offering any explanation for his presence on Martha's Vineyard off-season. Janice responded with the location of the cottage and reason for her visit nearly word-for-word what she'd told Shane. Was that story too rehearsed? He narrowed his eyes on her, but her gaze up at the officer was bland.

"So, Ms. Swenson, you'll be here however long it takes to renovate and sell the old Moran place." The policeman thrust her license back at her.

"That would be correct." Her chin went up as she accepted the plastic.

"Good luck. You'll need it."

"Why do you say that?" Janice's tone climbed half an octave.

"Maybe this heir you're working for didn't explain the place's reputation to you."

"I've heard vague rumors. Can you elaborate?"

"I don't deal in old sea tales." The officer extended Shane's license toward him. "And you—how long will you be here?"

"I'm assisting Ms. Swenson."

Shane took his identification and slipped it back into his wallet. Let the policeman make what he would about that statement. At least it gave him a better cover than beach bum. He was grateful for that much.

"All right." The officer nodded. "You two take care now." Then the man turned on his heel and sauntered toward Bill, who was scraping the bottom of his bowl with his spoon, grinning as though he had no cares.

"The nerve of the officer!" Janice's outrage drew Shane's attention. "Making it sound like our own carelessness nearly got us killed. There's not a chance on earth I'll talk to *him* about our suspicions of sabotage."

High color flushed her cheeks as she tossed a thick strand of her chestnut ponytail behind her shoulder. Green fire blazed from enormous eyes as full lips firmed above a strong but delicately rounded chin. How she managed to perfectly meld ferocity with beauty was a gift few women possessed.

Shane forcibly swallowed his heart back into place. No way could he get sidetracked by a galloping attraction to a woman he knew almost nothing about. Her presence added an unexpected and unwelcome complication to his quest. He needed to find out as much as he could about her as quickly as possible. What were the chances he'd like what he discovered?

FIVE

"Essie Mae didn't seem to think I'd have a problem finding a buyer for the property," Janice said to Shane as he drove toward the lumberyard in Vineyard Haven. Did the worry gnawing her soul show in her voice? "Of course, she assumed it would be an off-islander who would snap it up as a summer place."

Shane shrugged. "She seemed to figure Officer Mitch would be on our side in the matter of the accident, too, but I guess she was wrong on two counts. I felt grilled to well done, and he and Bill Beasley seemed awfully chummy when we left."

Janice shook her head. "Essie Mae could be one of those eternal optimists. Can't fault her for looking on the bright side."

"Maybe she knows some of those 'sea tales' about the cottage that the officer mentioned."

"I have mixed feelings about hearing the specifics." Janice dropped her gaze and brushed at smudges of dirt on her jeans. A few oil stains from her roll across the road might not come out in the wash. So far, the island had been hard on her body and her wardrobe.

Any tales about Moran Cottage would have to do with prior occupants, and no, she didn't want to hear them. No need to add to the load of vicarious guilt her heritage laid upon her. But maybe she needed to listen as a matter of self-preservation. Could the property's past have anything to do with present danger? Maybe she hadn't been recognized as a Moran, but simply an intruder. Why would anyone want to scare her away from the cottage? Too many questions and not enough answers. Yet.

"Well, Shane Gillum," she said as she lifted her head and gazed at her volunteer chauffeur and would-be handyman, "what sort of lumber shall we get for that treacherous porch?"

"Are you looking for wood or man-made composite material? The composite might stand up better to oceanside conditions."

"No synthetics will go into this building—well, other than modern appliances. A vintage presentation will be a selling point."

"Gotcha, Ms. Realtor." His sidelong glance teased her.

A grin escaped, even as she clamped down on the flutter of her pulse. The guy had lethal eyes with naturally long, thick lashes that women made up their faces to achieve.

"I kind of liked 'Tuff' better," she told him.

He let out his deep laugh. "Me, too. It fits."

She shook her head. "Not so much. I just put on a good show."

Shane hummed and rolled one shoulder. He might be skeptical about her disclaimer, but she knew all too well it was true. Not that she was going to argue with him about the matter. Let him harbor his illusions.

"Something pressure-treated but with a rough, knotty grain might be the type of wood you're looking for," he said. "You get natural-appearing durability."

"There we go. Now we're on the right track."

They discussed building material the rest of the way to the lumberyard, where they made their purchases in one accord. A helpful sales associate, working through a very up-to-date computer system, drew up electronically generated plans for a new porch that fit the specified dimensions. Even so, the process of selecting everything right down to a skill saw, hammer and nails took a few hours. The yard manager promised to have the material and tools delivered that afternoon.

As they turned to leave, he trotted after them. "What say I send along a coupla guys to help dismantle the old porch, shore up the roof overhang, and haul the old stuff away? It'll only add a hundred bucks to the cost, provided we get to keep the old wood for sale to crafters and folks looking for fireplace kindling."

Janice looked toward Shane and he shrugged. "In college, I spent a summer working as a carpenter's assistant, so I should do fine renovating a simple porch but any way to jump-start the project might be handy."

"I agree." Janice nodded to the yard manager. "Send the demo crew, will you?"

The guy grinned and waved as they went out the door.

Just past noon they pulled up to the cottage on the hill. Janice frowned. The old place showed its age and neglect. It was up to her—and now Shane—to transform it into a vintage showplace. Had she chomped off the proverbial bite too large to chew?

As Janice got out of the Jeep, an ocean wind snatched her ponytail and tossed it to the front of her shoulder. The same breeze sighed through the eaves of the cottage in a long, low moan—as if the property mourned its disreputable provenance. She shivered. A bright coat of paint would do a lot to cheer up the place, but would a facelift ever be enough to erase the stain of the Moran name?

A hand settled on her shoulder and she jerked.

The hand withdrew. "Sorry. Didn't mean to startle you."

Janice turned to find Shane staring at her with arms raised and a lopsided grin on his face.

"No, I'm sorry for being such a Nervous Nelly. I don't mind telling you, this place has already got me spooked. I can't be done with this project fast enough."

Shane nodded. "I'll do my part to make that happen. We can't really get started on the porch until the crew and the supplies get here. While we wait, I'd like to take a look at that cellar step that gave way beneath you yesterday."

Janice ratcheted in a long breath. "I'd appreciate your doing that. If there's anything suspicious about it, let me know. I'd hate to think whoever sabotaged the roofing material has been inside the cottage, also."

"Me, too." His gaze was grim.

"In the meantime," Janice said in a deliberately lighter tone, "I'll throw together a couple of sandwiches so we can be fueled up and ready for action by the time the crew from the lumberyard gets here."

"You're on." He grinned. "Can I leave Atlas in the kitchen with you?"

"Absolutely." Janice grinned back. "He might even fall heir to a few tidbits of cold cuts that just happen to land on the floor…if you don't mind, that is."

Shane cocked his head. His adorable expression of mock severity stole oxygen from Janice's lungs. Why did this guy have to be so impossibly cute?

"As long as the evidence is completely consumed," he pronounced gravely, "what the owner cannot verify may remain forever a secret between the gracious hostess and grateful canine."

Janice spluttered a laugh. "Come on then, Atlas."

She motioned and the dog wagged his entire hind end as he let out a soft bark and trotted after her. Visions of Shane Gillum's many attractive expressions danced in her head as she trod up the steps.

"Watch out for that broken board!"

The cry from behind froze her in midstep. "Yikes! My mind is definitely elsewhere."

She glanced over her shoulder at Shane, who was shaking his head with arms folded across his chest. Her cheeks heated. "Thanks."

Good thing he had no idea that he was the chief distraction in her thoughts. What was the matter with her? She had much larger issues deserving her attention than a good-looking Good Samaritan she would never see again after this brief sojourn meant to sever the last of the family strings.

Stifling a sigh, she stepped over the faulty planking and entered the cottage. Traces of burned-bagel odor remained, along with a hint of that stuffiness a place acquires after being shut up for a long time. "We need to open those windows wider for the rest of the day. Air this place out. A new owner won't be interested in something that smells like an old attic."

"I'm on it," Shane said.

Janice retired to the kitchen as the sounds of window frames sliding upward combined with a tuneless whistle. At least someone was cheerful. Her mood had drooped just from walking through the door and seeing what needed to be done.

"Say!" Shane called. "There's a van that says Jay Harder Plumbing on the side pulling up out here."

"Great!" she called. "I can almost feel the bliss of that hot shower."

Shane answered with a chuckle. "Assuming the water heater is housed in the basement, I'll escort Jay down there to get started. It'll give me a good excuse for checking out that missing step."

"Thanks!" Janice began distributing slices of bread onto paper plates.

Making sandwiches with the friendly Atlas sniffing around for treats and adoring her with his eyes lifted her spirits. *Come on, girl,* she chided herself. *Not that long ago, you fought a killer and didn't back down. Maybe you didn't win the fight and almost lost your life, but hey, God sent a rescuer.* Warm gratitude rose in Janice's heart toward that unlikely hero, her best friend's soon-to-be-husband. Who would have guessed that a guy she'd disliked on sight—for irrational reasons, she now realized—would save her and said best friend from freezing to death in a crawl space after being kidnapped by a serial killer? Janice hauled in a long breath and let it out slowly. *God's with you now, too. Shane might even be another unlikely hero sent to help you. Get your act together, stay focused, and you'll get through this.*

The sounds of heavy male footfalls and deep voices accompanied her preparations. A creak from the hallway betrayed that the men had opened the hatch in the floor. Lips pressed together, Janice added handfuls of chips and crisp red apples to the lunch plates. Breath half bated and ears cocked toward the hallway, she deposited the knife she'd used to spread mayonnaise on the sandwiches into the ceramic sink. Hopefully, she would soon be able to do the small pile of dishes she'd accumulated.

She picked up half of one of her sandwiches and squinted at it. Should she add pickles? Since when was she so indecisive about something so simple? Since coming here, apparently.

"Tuff?" Shane's tentative almost wincing tone turned her away from the counter.

He held out the faulty step board. "This is the way I found it."

What she saw—or rather, what she didn't see—weakened her knees and loosened her fingers. The sandwich plopped to the floor.

Gasping in a breath, Janice wilted against the counter. "The intruder *was* in my house!"

"*Your* house?" Shane's question exploded with more bite to it than he would have liked.

Janice blinked at him, disoriented. "The place where I'm staying." She waved as if batting at something annoying but inconsequential. "You know. Like you'd say about your hotel room if you returned to find it ransacked."

"Oh." Shane cleared his throat and dropped his gaze. He seriously needed to get a leash on his suspicions—unless, of course, he was letting her off the hook too easily. Could she know more about this place and the Morans than she'd let on?

He fingered the lighter-colored area and nail holes where the absent support strip would have been on the bottom of the step board. "Someone took this off, and I think they weakened the nails in the sides—possibly with the same saw they used to tamper with the roof."

"But how did they get into the house? Why?"

"Answers to those questions remain to be found, but you can't stay here anymore."

"Move miles away to a hotel or B and B and let some saboteur have free run of the place? I don't think so, Mr. Gillum."

That ferocious beauty glinted at him from her perfect face, and Shane firmed his jaw against the pull of admiration. "Yes, *you* move to a guest facility where you can rest in peace and safety, and with your permission, *I* will stay here."

Her jaw dropped but no sound came out.

"Trying to find a rationalization to refute my logic? Sorry, there isn't one." If he didn't want to cold cock the jerk who'd booby-trapped this place he'd shake the person's hand for offering him this opportunity to search the house while he kept watch over the property.

Janice closed her mouth and narrowed her eyes. Was the woman going to buck even this simple logic? Unbelievable!

"Oookaaay." The word drawled low and long from her lips. "I'll make you a deal, sugar."

He didn't figure the mild endearment meant anything more than a Southern habit of speech. Or maybe there was actually a slight bite to it, not implying sweetness at all.

"What's the deal?"

Her lips tilted upward in a smile he could only describe as sly and determined.

"You and Atlas may spend your nights here, and I will sleep at your place. Apparently it's within walking distance, and that's what I want. I plan to spend every waking moment right here, getting this property ready to unload."

"Deal." Shane stuck out his hand.

Janice lifted her right hand, palm out. "I'm not finished. I don't expect the same daily time commitment from you, as I'm sure you have antiques to hunt. Also, I'm going to install the landline phone you suggested so we can reach help at any given moment."

"Excellent." Shane kept his hand out. "My place already has a landline, and until this project is done, I don't mind spending significant time here. I'm beginning to feel invested."

She smiled and slid her palm into his. The warm contact flooded up his arm straight to his heart. She gave his fingers a squeeze and released him. He felt the loss. What was up with that?

Stuffing his hands in his jeans' pockets, Shane's gaze dropped toward his dog. Atlas sat on his haunches, licking his whiskery jaw. No trace of the fallen sandwich remained on the floor.

"Half rations for you tonight, buddy." Shane shook his head, suppressing a grin.

"Guess I'd better make another sandwich." Janice laughed.

They were standing in the kitchen, polishing off the sandwiches and being serenaded by clinking and clanking noises from the plumber at work in the bathroom, when a honk from outside announced the arrival of a delivery truck. Through the window, Shane observed a crew of three men pile out of the cab. If his dad wasn't a Three Stooges fan, he would have missed the entertaining resemblance.

"What are you grinning about?"

Janice's question drew his attention to her licking the last of the bread crumbs from her fingers.

"Let's hope these guys don't act like the ones they look like." He jerked a thumb toward the trio beginning to unload lumber from the rear of the truck. "Our work crewmen are dead ringers for Larry, Curly and Moe."

"Who?"

"Never mind. Just kick my shin on the sly if I start to refer to any of them by one of those names. I'd better get outside and give them a hand."

"I'll come along to direct operations and generally get in the way."

Laughing companionably, they went out the door. Far from getting in the way, Janice proved savvy about how to organize materials for handy access. As they unloaded supplies, and she directed where to lay them out on the ground in front of the cabin, Shane had no problem bowing to her guidance.

Not so with the lumberyard crew. They weren't lazy, but didn't appear overly industrious, either, and from the terse bits of conversation no sense of humor peeped from among the three of them. If any slapstick erupted, it might be him smacking the guy he'd mentally dubbed Moe—the one with the long, lean face and bowl-cut hair. The guy rolled his eyes every time Janice said a word.

At last, the truck was empty. The Moe-dude thrust toward Shane a clipboard holding a manifest of the delivered goods. The pen pointing at him from Moe's other hand suggested he was expected to sign.

Shane took a step backward and cocked his thumb at Janice. "She's the boss. It might be smart if you'd figure out which side of the bread holds the butter."

Moe's dark brows crunched together. "Say what? We already had lunch, ayah."

The buzz-cut Curly sniggered. What do you know? A sense of humor and he had the high-pitched tone of the real Curly. Sober-faced, the bald-on-top, bushy-on-the-sides Larry took the clipboard and pen from his colleague and handed it to Janice. She smiled and thanked him as she signed, graciousness personified.

"Now, be very careful while you remove the existing porch," she said as she handed the manifest back to Larry. "There may be unaddressed roofing issues, and we don't need anyone hurt."

"Thanks, ma'am. We'll exercise due caution." The guy's accent was more New York than New England, but at least he didn't have a Neanderthal attitude.

Maybe Moe was the only one with the sexist issues. The guy confirmed Shane's suspicions as he grumbled under his breath while they prepared to remove the porch.

"—does she think we are? Amateurs? Bossy female..."

That was the extent of the words Shane made out, but they were plenty to bring a scowl to his face as he hefted a crowbar to begin prying boards away from the frame.

Lord, is it unchristian of me to wish I could use this to pry the top of the guy's head off and pour in some sense?

Janice disappeared around the side of the house, and Shane's gut tensed. Should he be concerned about her wandering around the place on her own? In a little while, sounds emerging from the open windows betrayed that she'd gone inside through the kitchen entrance. He peered through the front-room window and caught her humming a currently popular praise tune as she rubbed a rag over the woodwork on the mantelpiece. She glanced toward the window and froze with a tiny squeak then her shoulders slumped and she waved.

"Sorry," Shane mouthed and bent back to his task.

After her mysterious intruder experience, seeing his face in the same window must have given her quite a start until her brain processed his identity. If he ever found out who was haunting this place that person might need to worry about answering to him.

Shane popped a board loose with extra vigor.

Maybe *he* needed to worry about the depth of his antagonism toward this threat to Janice. Of course, the threat might be connected to people who were racing him to find what Shane sought. In that case, maybe his reaction to the saboteur was colored by guilty feelings about keeping his objective from her. Maybe his protective drive was actually about conscience rather than attraction to this woman who revealed herself more and more as a fine and decent Christian person.

Sure, and maybe the seagulls swooping and screeching above would turn into fish and the sky into the sea. *Face it, buddy. There's more danger here than some crooks who are after the same thing you are and will kill to get it.* A wind gust from ocean-side enveloped Shane, and sweat chilled on his body. He suppressed a shiver as he stood straight and stretched a kink from his back.

"Shane?"

He turned toward the somber, masculine voice. The Larry lumberyard employee—Shane seemed to remember his real name was Chuck—held out a broken board.

"What's up?" Shane eyed the shredded ends of the board halves.

"This wood isn't rotten," Larry-Chuck stated flatly. "True, the wood is pretty badly weathered, but if you didn't care about how the porch looked, you could have probably replaced the one board and left the rest alone."

Shane's eyes widened. A lumberyard employee discouraging them from going through with a project? This guy was honest to a fault.

"What do you mean?"

"Somebody used an ax on this." He shook the two halves of the board that Atlas had stuck his leg through.

Shane hissed a breath between his teeth. More mean and petty sabotage. How was he going to break the news to Janice? She was jumpy enough already. Maybe it was time for him to do whatever was necessary to send her packing. Yes, but what?

Later that evening Shane went back to his cabin to take a shower. Afterward, hair still damp, he picked up his cordless handset and punched in a number. He had to go through some rigmarole with the person who initially answered, but finally the one he wanted to talk to came on the line.

"Hey, Dad."

"Hi, son."

At the gentle endearment in his father's voice, Shane swallowed against a lump that rose in his throat. He and his father hadn't been close when Shane was growing up, but recent crises had thrust them into a situation where father suddenly depended on son. A new and precious trust had sprung up between them, and Shane wasn't about to disappoint his dad.

"I've got access to the cottage. You're hardly going to believe this, but the heir sent a Realtor to handle renovation and sale of the place. Hasn't even bothered to put in an appearance. I'm helping the Realtor get the place spruced up."

"Resourceful young man."

Dad's proud grin came through his tone and Shane's heart swelled. Affirmation had been hard to come by in his childhood years.

"I always knew you had it in you," his father continued. "We'll expose the truth yet and take those scoundrels down."

"As much as I'd love that, I'm more concerned about getting you out of there. They treating you all right?"

Dad chuckled, but the sound was a little tired, more than a little sad. "I'm an old duffer around here. Nobody pays me much mind if I keep my head down and do what I'm told. They've got a library, so I read. Some limited access to computers, so I research things. Did you know that Moran Cottage has a reputation?"

"I've been discovering that."

"Everything from a pirate hideout to a bootlegger's pit stop."

"No surprises there."

"Doesn't that suggest anything to you?"

Shane settled at the kitchen table. "Are you hinting at secret passages and hidden rooms?"

"Bingo!"

"I'm sounding the place out for those. The cottage has a pretty interesting cellar. I'll take a closer look."

"You do that. Also, look up this news article online." Dad dictated a web address and Shane jotted it down on a scrap of paper from a notepad. "Reggie may have framed me up nice and neat—some thank you for over twenty-five years of faithful work—but he sure got what was coming to him. His plane was more than likely sabotaged, but no one cares." His father stopped and cleared his throat. "Sorry. I'm starting to sound vindictive. This place is wearing me down. Feels so hopeless."

"Hang in there, Dad. I'm getting close." *Please, God, let that be the truth.* "The Almighty is the only one who could have arranged for me to have such free access to the cottage. I don't even have to sneak around. I'll be spending the night there tonight. Alone."

"The Realtor got himself a cushy bed at a B and B?"

"Herself. But no, she's taking my cabin while I guard her place."

"Guard?"

"Some hinky things have been happening over there. I don't know what to think. Are you positive the Morans don't know Reggie stashed the records on his Martha's Vineyard property?"

Several heartbeats of silence passed. "Who knows what the mob knows?"

Shane frowned. Not a comforting response, but he wouldn't want anything less than the truth.

"Let's put it this way," Dad continued, "*I* know only because I ran out to the plane to have him sign a document just before he took off that last day, and you know my photographic memory. I got a gander of his instrument settings. After everything hit the fan, and I had reason to be suspicious, I looked up the destination. It was the latitude and longitude of the cottage property. Exactly. I've checked out online satellite images and Reggie *could* have landed his small plane in the field behind the cottage, did what he needed to do, and then take off again. Interestingly enough, that pit stop wasn't anywhere in his logged flight plan, which was completely bogus anyway, and as far as I know, the flight plan is the only information available to anyone—police or mobster."

"Okay." Shane jerked a nod, though his father couldn't see it. "Good enough. I'm on it. Won't rest until you're out of there."

"That's my boy! Whatever you do, son, keep your head down. Don't let anyone know who you are. I wish I hadn't asked you to start poking around in the first place, but it's too late now. One perk in the joint, if you can call it that, is loads of free scuttlebutt floating around. Not a lot else to do but gossip. I found out who the Morans hired to put the hit on you."

Shane's skin crawled. Twice while he was still Seth Grange, a bullet with his name on it had streaked toward his unsuspecting head. Twice some total fluke had saved him. First it was an unexpected slip in a puddle of coffee a patron had spilled, and the bullet splatted harmlessly into the side of the Starbucks. A week or so later, he was walking through a local park, and a kid's soccer ball whapped his knees and bowled him over just as a bullet lodged itself in a tree. That's when he decided he had to resign from being Seth and start being Shane. And that was also when his father remembered what he'd seen in Reggie's plane, put two-and-two together about Moran Cottage and sent him to Martha's Vineyard. There was no reason to think the Morans were on to the place, but then who was messing with them here and why?

"Go on," Shane-Seth invited his dad.

"The name is Norman Marks. They call him The Marks Man, and with good reason. He always fulfills his contracts. Word is, he's raging mad about the disappearance of his latest mark. He's put up a reward of his personal money to find you."

"Won't he come after you to try to get my location?"

"Already sent someone. Him or the Morans. Doesn't matter which. Seems I've got me an interesting roommate. Lucky Labria from the Luciano Family."

"The Morans' age-old rivals?"

"The same. I'm wedged in deep with a clan of them stuck in here with me. They're rooting for you to take their enemies down, and keeping me safe and out of Moran hands is high on their to-do list. If the Lucianos didn't practically own this prison, I wouldn't dare talk to you on the phone. Say the word, and I don't doubt they'd send some muscle to the island to help you."

Shane shuddered. "No thanks, Dad. I'm not interested in letting one mob help me put another one away."

"Probably a bad move anyway. A Luciano or two hovering around you would throw up a red flag as to your whereabouts."

"I'm glad you're safe anyway."

Dad laughed. "If I didn't know better, I'd think that God of yours is looking after me just like He does you. Ironic, huh?"

"God's mercy, Dad. It's new every morning."

"Well, you just keep believing that. One of us has to. Now, remember, when you get your hands on that evidence that will clear *me* and incriminate *them,* make sure that *I'm* the first one to see it. I want to be the one to turn it in. Got that?"

"Sure, Dad, I heard you the first ten times you reminded me." Shane chuckled.

He didn't agree with his father on that procedure, but he wasn't going to waste time arguing. The extra step between the discovery of the records and turning it in to the cops seemed like unnecessary risk to Shane.

Somebody hollered in the background and Dad said his time was up.

"I love you, son."

Shane nearly choked up again. He'd been waiting his whole life to hear those words on a regular basis from his father. "Love you, too, Dad."

They said goodbye and Shane clicked off his phone, heart heavy. Regardless of how his father tried to make light of life behind bars, prison was a dangerous place to be. Shane had to get him out of there. Dad wasn't ready yet to meet his Maker.

SIX

Janice jerked awake in the pitch black, shivering, and lunged upright in bed. Sore muscles protested the sudden movement. Where was she?

Clearly not in that frigid crawl space where her Colorado attacker had stashed her and her best friend in the dead of a Rocky Mountain winter. Even though her attempted murderer was cold in the grave himself, the event was not yet far enough in the past to cease waking her up with bad dreams saturated in bitter chill and claustrophobia.

A faint odor of lime and bay rum brought present memory tumbling back. She was sleeping in Shane's cabin a quarter mile down the beach from her cottage. Janice pressed a palm to her forehead and winced at a twinge from the gash on the top of her head. The threat from a faceless saboteur must have agitated memories of experiences she was trying to forget. She'd come to Martha's Vineyard to heal. Apparently a new enemy had other plans for her.

How was Shane up at the cottage? Were he and Atlas experiencing an uneventful night?

Heavy silence and darkness pressed in on Janice, accenting the sound of her breathing. A hum suddenly commenced and she jerked then huffed out a long sigh. What was the matter with her? The noise was only the refrigerator motor kicking in. A very normal sound, only her nerves were nowhere normal pitch.

Maybe she should have yielded to Shane's pressure to take Atlas with her for the night. She'd refused to do so, figuring he needed the insurance of a sharp nose and swift bark at skulking strangers more than she did. At least if she'd taken the dog, she'd have had a friendly presence to take the edge off the pervasive loneliness that saturated her soul. She could bury her fingers in warm fur and be assured of unconditional acceptance.

God? Are You still there for me?

She and the Almighty had been going through a rough patch lately. Or more honestly, she'd been having the rough patch. She constantly assured herself that He would never leave or forsake her, that He was as close as her next breath, whether she felt Him or not. But it would sure be nice to feel those Everlasting Arms. A sense of distance persisted and she didn't know how to fix it.

Letting out a sigh, Janice checked the digital read-out on the clock: 3:00 a.m. Too early to be up and about, but she wasn't likely to fall back to sleep quickly. She rose and, guided by a hallway night-light, padded to the bathroom. So pleasant to have running water for her hands and face. Poor Shane, making due with primitive. At least he'd been able to come back here and take his shower before turning in for the night at her place.

The plumber had not had good news. The water heater would need to be replaced, as well as all the piping into the bathroom. The pipes that led to the kitchen were newer and usable. To get everything in working order, he would need to order a few special fittings that would come in on the ferry from the mainland within the next few days. Until then, they would have cold water in the kitchen only, but that was the extent of the liquid amenities.

Oh, well, heating a pan of water on the kitchen stove allowed for dishes to be done, and both she and Shane could arrange to have their showers at his place. She was fervently looking forward to one of those this morning, but not yet. If she hopped under the spray now, she'd be awake for the day.

She went to the kitchen, grabbed a minibottle of water from the refrigerator and adjourned to the modest living room. Atop a small table flanked by a pair of chairs, a tiny red light blinked at her from a closed laptop. She lifted the lid and squinted at the sign-in screen. Even if she knew Shane's password, would she have the gall to access his files? For her own peace of mind, not to mention her trust level in Shane, she might. Too many questions lurked in the corners of her consciousness about his motives and odd reactions to things such as police involvement.

Shutting the laptop shifted its position slightly and the small light on its side revealed a corner of a piece of paper. With the tip of a finger, Janice drew the paper forth. It was only a scrap ripped from a larger sheet, mostly blank except for some writing on it she couldn't read in the dark. Reluctant to turn on a light, she picked up the scrap and carried it to the kitchen and read the text inside the open refrigerator door.

It looked to be the web address for an article in an online newspaper, the *Buffalo Times*. Did that mean Buffalo, New York, or was it some kind of Wild West newspaper? She wouldn't know until she accessed the web herself.

Mulling, she put the paper back where she'd found it. Then she returned to bed and pulled the covers up to her chin. She'd probably just toss and turn, but the off chance of a few more hours of shut-eye was worth a shot.

Why did she care that Shane was reading an online newspaper? The web reference was probably innocuous and had nothing to do with his presence on the island or with her. Then again, the article could prove crucial to understanding him—or even pertain to her well-being.

Now she was on pins and needles to find out. She'd never fall asleep…

"Janice!"

At the urgent masculine call, her eyes popped open. Bright slices of sunlight filtered through the blinds onto the bedspread. What do you know? She'd slept again. Apparently for hours. She heard her name again.

"I'm here. I'm fine," she answered.

Footfalls approached the bedroom and Shane's head poked around the doorway. His expression was sober. "You didn't show up for breakfast so I felt a little scared. Thought I'd better check on you. Glad you got some extra shut-eye."

"What time is it?"

Her glance at the bedside clock coincided with his answer.

"Nearly 10:00 a.m."

"Whoa! I really did sleep in. I didn't mean to."

"You're entitled." Shane grinned at her.

Janice sat up, hugging the covers to her chest. Not that her pajamas weren't modest anyway, but it was a little weird to have a guy looking at you waking up in *his* bed. Shane retreated. A pang of guilt smote her. Really, he was such a nice fellow, why was she suspicious of him?

Atlas had no such inclination to respect her privacy. He trotted over to the bedside and reared up with his front paws on the mattress. She shooed him off as she rose to her feet. She gave him the scratch behind the ears he was looking for and then reached for her robe.

"I'll clean up quick and be over in a half hour."

"No hurry," Shane said. "I'm working on the porch. That project will probably take me the rest of the day. See you."

"Wait!" Janice belted on her robe as she hurried out into the hallway.

Shane stood by the front door, gazing at her expectantly.

"Did you have a decent night's sleep?" she asked.

He shrugged with a half smile. "That blow-up mattress is pretty comfortable. Plus, our unfriendly neighborhood saboteur must have had the night off."

"That's good. I'm very relieved." She let out a breath. "I see you have your laptop here. Do you get internet service?"

"Through the landline. It's not very fast, but so far it's seemed reliable."

"Good. I think I'll have that connected up at the cottage, too. I'll phone in the order from here before I leave."

Shane gave her a thumbs-up as he went out the door, whistling for Atlas. The dog bounded after his master, but awarded her a backward look as he left the cabin. Those big brown eyes tugged on her heart almost as much as his master's big blue ones. That was not good. Not good at all. Since she categorically would not—could not tell Shane who she really was, there was no hope for extending the relationship beyond this brief sojourn on the island.

If only being around Shane didn't feel so right.

Kneeling on the new porch that was slowly taking shape, Shane placed a nail in position and brought the hammer down. A twinge of pain shot up his arm as the head nicked the edge of his poorly positioned thumb. He grimaced and gave his hand a shake. A carpenter he wasn't, but he was committed to this project and would see it through.

At least he could feel good that Janice got extra rest last night. She probably wouldn't have slept a wink if she'd had a clue what he was doing here in the wee hours. This subterfuge business was hard on a guy who prized honesty.

If only he could find what he came for. But free range of the cottage hadn't yielded any results, though he'd roamed about tapping walls and floors for hollow hiding places, perhaps a concealed safe, until after 2:00 a.m. By then he'd lost the battle to keep his eyes open and his head clear. He couldn't afford to give up or get discouraged though. He had to continue the search…and the identity masquerade.

As long as his enemies regarded Janice and him as ignorant interlopers to be scared off the place rather than simply eliminated, their lives were as safe as they could be when tangling with a major crime family. Of course, he hadn't totally written off the thought that the arranged accidents weren't actually connected to his search. Petty mayhem wasn't usually on the Morans' playlist. Maybe they *weren't* on to this place. Yet, at least. Maybe someone else wanted Janice to leave and the property abandoned. But why?

It was nerve-racking not to be sure of the enemy's identity. As nerve-racking as trying to keep his own identity concealed.

Deep barks brought Shane's head up. Atlas had leaped from a lounging spot at the base of the porch frame and was racing toward a tall, willowy figure in a pale blue sweatshirt and jeans making her way up the incline from the beach. Shane waved toward Janice and she returned the gesture. She wasn't close enough for him to tell if she was smiling or not.

Shane mentally kicked himself. Why did her smiles matter to him?

Janice arrived at the cottage red-faced and puffing.

"Maybe you should drive back and forth between the places," he said.

"No way," she huffed. "I need the exercise. Clearly. Since biking is out of the question—" she lifted her casted arm "—and I don't have time to join a local fitness club, walking and climbing are perfect. I haven't been this out of shape since…" Her words trailed off and a shadow passed over her face. "Well, since ever."

What was she holding back? Shane bottled the question behind his tongue.

"No sling today?"

She shrugged. "It's in my back pocket. If the wrist starts to ache or my hand to swell, I'll put it on. But I'd like the use of my fingers as much as possible."

"Don't push yourself too hard, Tuff. You'll delay your healing."

Janice scrunched her face at him then offered a smile. "Heard and understood, Mr. Paramedic. Also, I did the prudent thing and reported the sabotage out here. Hopefully they'll send someone other than Officer Mitch." She wrinkled her nose. "The police station in Edgartown is dispatching an officer to take a look at the evidence of tampering, and the phone company says the underground wires were laid years ago from the road to here. They only have to switch on the service, which they will do sometime today or tomorrow. That's as close as I could pin them down."

Shane chuckled. "That's utility companies for you."

"It'll be good to have internet and phone service, but it's only one line so we can't talk on the telephone and be on the web at the same time."

"Way better than total isolation."

"You got that right."

The purr of an engine drew closer and a police cruiser drove into view, heading for the gravel parking area beside the cottage.

Shane let out a low whistle. "That was fast." He rose from his hands and knees.

Janice nodded, staring toward the cruiser. "They must have had someone in the area."

The police vehicle stopped and a uniform emerged. This cop was about Officer Mitch's height, but lanky and female. She opened the rear door of the car and a bulky German shepherd leaped out. Shane's pulse moved into overdrive, sweat popped onto his brow, and he suddenly had difficulty drawing his next breath. Bunching his hands into fists, he eased toward the front door of the cottage.

Atlas barked and moved toward the other dog, but Janice grabbed his collar. "Atlas is a teddy bear," she said to the officer. "But I'm not sure how friendly your dog might be with other dogs."

"Not very, I'm afraid. Don't worry about it. I just let him out to do his business. I'll put him back in the car in a sec."

For Shane the "second" stretched into what felt like at least an hour as he stood sweating on the porch. *Breathe, man, breathe!* he mentally barked at himself. *Remember the techniques you used when you were acclimating to Atlas.*

Yeah, but Atlas was a friendly pooch. The police dog was trained to take people down. *Trained.* The word reverberated through him. The dog would not attack unless ordered to do so, and Shane was not a target. Taking command of himself, despite his irrational terror, he put one foot ahead of the other and left the porch. He arrived at the bottom of the steps as the officer shut the squad car door behind the dog. An invisible iron band sprang loose from his chest and he sucked in a deep breath.

"You're afraid of dogs?" Janice's speculative eye on him heated his neck. "I never would have guessed."

"That's good news." Shane sent her a grin. "That breed of dog in particular always throws me for a loop. Took me six weeks to recover from a German Shepherd attack when I was a kid. Lots of stitches."

"Wow! Sorry to hear that. Impressive that you didn't run into the cottage and lock the door."

"I'm a little proud of myself, yes."

Shane withheld further comment. The police officer had fixed them with a steady gaze and was striding their way. Atlas let out a low woof, but this time Shane grabbed his collar as the animal tried to lunge toward the potential new friend who might scratch behind his ears. Under other circumstances, the dog's tail-drooping disappointment might have drawn a grin from Shane.

Eyeing the large canine that whined and wagged its hind end, the cop halted a few feet from them. "I'm Officer Pat Harkins. Someone called in about an intruder and vandalism?"

Janice introduced herself. Shane gave his name. "And this is Atlas," he added. "Pet him, and you'll have a pest for life."

Officer Pat chuckled. "As you can see, I like dogs. I'll take my chances." She stepped forward, let Atlas sniff her fingers, and then made one pooch's day with a thorough ear scratch.

Shane couldn't suppress a smile and Janice laughed.

"What do you have for me?" The officer crossed her arms, suddenly all business.

"The day before yesterday—the day I arrived at the place—I saw a trespasser on my porch," Janice said. "That was right after I took a tumble down the cellar steps, which we discovered later was actually a booby trap."

"How do you know it was a trap?"

"We have the evidence right here." Shane hefted a plastic garbage sack that had been lying beside the rebuilt porch steps. "One chopped porch board, a sawed roof tile and a partially dismantled wooden step."

"So you're reporting more than one act of sabotage, and you have solid proof?" The officer's gaze brightened.

Did the policewoman sound unusually eager? Shane

angled a look at Janice. Her brows were puckered. Had she noticed the same thing?

"Let's see the items." Officer Pat reached for the bag.

Shane surrendered it. Why he should feel reluctant to do so, he couldn't fathom. By now he should be getting used to the feeling that more was going on than he knew about.

The officer took slow and careful time examining each item, the oddly striated roof tile, the ragged ends of the chopped porch boards and the weakened stair step. Several times she grunted or muttered, "I'll be" or "Would you look at that!"

Next to him, Janice shifted from foot to foot. Shane tamped down his stomach flutters. He didn't have anything to be nervous about, did he? Unless Officer Mitch had done some digging and discovered that Shane wasn't Shane. But why would he have done that? And wouldn't this officer have questioned his identity at once if his false identification was common knowledge in the police department?

Finally, Officer Pat stowed the evidence in the bag and looked them in the eyes. "I'll have to take this stuff with me."

"Are you going to dust it for fingerprints or do other lab tests, Officer Harkins?" Janice asked.

"Officer Pat will do, or just Pat. Sorry, Ms. Swenson, material like this doesn't retain fingerprints very well."

"It's Janice." She smiled and the officer responded in kind. "You'll keep it in an evidence locker then until the culprit is caught? Maybe then you can compare tool marks or something."

"That would be the hoped-for conclusion to the matter."

Shane leaned forward. "But you consider that outcome a remote possibility?"

Officer Pat sighed. "If these items are all we have, yes, but if we can find out how the perpetrator gained entrance, we might discover more evidence to lead us to the culprit.

Actually, I'm tickled to have this much proof of flesh-and-blood involvement with shenanigans out at this place." She rattled the bag. "Some of the guys will need to see this to believe it."

"What's so unbelievable about dangerous pranking at a seemingly abandoned house?" Shane didn't bother to mask the irritation in his voice. Could nobody around here make sense?

"Local issue." Officer Pat waved a hand. "Based on one bogus report or another over the years, our department's been called out to this place more times than we've got fingers and toes. We never find anything amiss."

"Bogus reports?" Shane rocked back on his heels.

"You mean like the lights some fishermen claimed to see a few nights ago?" Janice asked. "A day or two before I arrived?"

"Stuff like the lights, yes." Pat nodded. "But that could well have been your saboteur at work. We didn't get called in on that one. I've only been on the Martha's Vineyard force for three years, but I've answered my share of calls on this place for lights or movement where there shouldn't be any. One time some neighbors down the road swore they heard something that sounded like an explosion in the middle of the night. I get here and just like every other time, nothing. The place was battened down and quiet like it should be."

"So I guess Moran Cottage has a pretty strong reputation," Janice said.

"You could say that."

Janice's mouth drooped and she stared at the ground. She was probably mentally watching her hopes to sell the place swirl down the drain that still wasn't working in her bathroom. Shane's heart squeezed. On instinct, he wound an arm around her shoulder and, surprisingly, she leaned into him.

Officer Pat dug a small pad of paper and a pencil from her uniform pocket. "Let me get a statement from each of you as to what happened, and then I'll case the place to see if I can find the intruder's access point."

"We haven't found anything," Janice said, "but I'd appreciate it if a professional would have a look." She straightened and Shane let his arm drop.

What had he been thinking, offering an embrace? He'd meant only to comfort her, right? Sure, and that was why he'd barely restrained his other arm from completing the hug. She'd felt too right that close to him. He didn't dare offer his shoulder again. What if he'd offended her?

Janice turned her head toward him and the light in her eyes was anything but offended. A new softness appeared around her lips and fresh warmth had melted some of the standoffish wariness that perennially lurked in the back of her gaze. Shane's mouth went dry. Apparently his impulsive sympathy—or was it something more?—had made a significant stride in earning her trust. That's what he wanted, wasn't it?

Why, then, did her looking at him as if she might like him as more than an assistant make him want to drop to his knees and confess everything to her? Maybe because she could be falling for someone who didn't exist, and he didn't like that one bit. If she was going to fall for someone, he wanted it to be the real him. How pathetic was that?

SEVEN

Janice could like this cop. Better to concentrate on positive vibes toward the local representative of the law than her sudden surge of warmth toward Shane. Right now, she didn't have time to examine why or how the man consistently and effortlessly slipped past her defenses.

Officer Pat fired probing questions at them, but the inquiries were pertinent and professional, without a taint of the bias Officer Mitch showed. Maybe her off-island police experience aided her objectivity. Janice finished her account of the cellar step collapsing beneath her and then getting bonked on the head by the falling roof tile as she was hollering for help at a passing beach-walker.

Officer Pat cocked a brown eye at Shane. "You're a paramedic, I hear. Lucky break for her."

Red crept up his neck. Why did he look as if the officer had just slapped him? Another hint that all was not well with Shane and his chosen profession? Janice had speculated about everything from personal problems to burn-out, but maybe he was hiding on Martha's Vineyard because he'd lost his job. Maybe he'd made a mistake or been accused of making one.

Shane Gillum might be mysterious and private and hurting in some way, though he tried to hide the inner turmoil, but he wasn't callous, or careless, or incompetent.

Perhaps he'd lost a patient under particularly heartrending circumstances. Janice had heard of such things sending medical professionals into full-blown retreat. One more reason to find out as much as she could about this man who was making inroads on her heart whether she wanted him to or not.

One side of his mouth tilted upward. "I suppose Officer Mitch has given the whole department an earful about the early tourists out here on this end of the island."

"Mitch? Nah." Pat chuckled. "But I don't mind revealing my source, and she wouldn't mind me revealing it, either."

"Essie Mae Furbish," Janice said.

Shane's voice said the same thing practically on top of hers, and they all grinned.

"Now, Mr. Gillum, let me get your account of matters," Officer Pat said.

"It's Shane," he answered. "I'll tell you whatever I can."

Ten minutes later Officer Pat tucked her pad into her pocket and fixed Janice with a questioning look. "Mind if I snoop around now?"

"Be my guest. The intruder didn't need access to the interior of the cottage to chop that porch board or saw that roof tile, but if anyone can show me how he got inside to sabotage the cellar step, I'll be grateful."

"Me, too," Shane said. "Need a hand, Officer?"

The ferocity in his gaze would scare Janice if it were directed at her. Maybe it should scare her that he felt so fierce on her behalf.

Officer Pat shook her head. "You two go back to what you were doing. If I find anything, I'll give a yell."

Shane's gaze followed the officer to her cruiser, where Pat deposited the sack of evidence, and then moved out of sight along the side of the house. Janice cleared her throat. Shane jerked his attention to her and his jawline visibly relaxed.

"Sorry. I'm kind of worked up."

"I see that. Can I get you a soda?"

"Sure, that would be great." His smile was forced, the look in his eyes distant and cold.

Stomach souring, Janice turned away and headed toward the side kitchen door. Maybe she was reading Shane entirely wrong. Perhaps his strong feelings about the situation had little to do with caring about her, but everything to do with his past—whatever had driven him to take refuge in a lonely little cabin on the corner of an island.

But if he'd wanted to be left alone to nurse his wounds, why had he volunteered to help her renovate the cottage? Too many things didn't add up about Shane Gillum. Janice needed to give her heart a stern lecture about feeling interest in a man she knew almost nothing about.

Forcibly unclenching his fists, Shane returned to work on the porch. He'd had to restrain his feet from running after the officer who was going to poke around the cottage. How strange would that have looked if he'd scurried along after her, uninvited and wringing his hands over what she might discover?

Sure, he wanted to get to the bottom of the intrusion and sabotage. He wanted—no, needed—Janice to be safe. But what if that process exposed things he desperately wanted to keep hidden, at least for a while yet? What if the diligent Officer Pat found the item he was looking for and took it into custody?

The policewoman was likable, but that didn't mean she was straight and narrow. How could he bear to watch helplessly while the last shred of evidence that would expose the truth disappeared down a black hole? Even if Pat was an honest cop, she might not realize the significance of what she held…or the dangers of turning it over to another officer or superiors who might be hand in glove with the mob.

No, Shane must find it first. For now, he had to keep his cool. Shane willed his hands steady and his aim accurate as he slammed nails into place on fresh boards. At least the physical activity provided an outlet for his frustrations.

"Shane!"

Janice's sharp tone stopped his hammer in midupswing. A drop of sweat from his forehead plopped onto the hand that held the nail. He turned to find her staring at him with wide eyes and a frown.

"I said your name three times." She extended a soda can toward him.

"Sorry about that." He laid down the hammer. "Woolgathering, I guess."

"Some pretty rough wool there." The green depths of her gaze searched him, invited him to explain.

He broke eye contact. "Someday I'd like to… Well, I hope I can—"

"Wa-hoo!"

A rebel yell that would have done Janice's Southern state proud sent an electric jolt through Shane. Apparently through Janice, too, because she took off at a run for the back of the cottage. Abandoning his soda, Shane trotted at her heels and Atlas at his. They found Officer Pat squatting beside a thickly matted clump of weeds crowding up against the foundation.

"Look here." She beamed up at them.

With a nightstick taken from her well-equipped belt, Pat pulled back the clump almost as one piece to reveal a narrow window well that led into the cellar. The pane of glass was missing.

Next to Shane, Janice gasped. "Whoever was at my window could have run around the house and dove into the cellar while I searched in vain. So my intruder was *inside* while I was outside. If I hadn't gone straight to the hospital for treatment, I could have run into him popping out the trap door in the hallway." She shuddered visibly.

"Or her," Shane said, restraining himself from wrapping an arm around her again.

"What?"

"That's right." Officer Pat rose. "A slender female or a kid would be the only ones who could fit through here. Even a skinny guy would have a hard time of it."

Janice nibbled a corner of her bottom lip. "It just seems like the person I saw outside my window was bulkier than that. Not tall, but wide."

Officer Pat delivered a wry smile. "When I started out my career in law enforcement, I was in the Wisconsin highway patrol. You have no idea how many accident scenes I've investigated where the motorists swore up and down they'd hit a gigantic buck deer, only to discover the corpse of a spotted fawn. When folks are startled or alarmed, the mind tends to magnify perceptions."

Janice nodded slowly, as if half convinced.

Shane frowned down into the hole. He wasn't stone-cold positive, but there might be another problem with the officer's apparent solution to the access dilemma.

"You don't know how tickled I am," the officer continued, "to finally have proof positive that goings-on out here can be blamed on flesh and blood, not spooks. A treasure-hunting teenager or even a small crew of them is involved, most likely."

"Treasure hunters?" Shane's brow knotted. That's all he needed. Money-hungry nut-jobs snooping around.

"Why would anyone think there's treasure around here?" Janice said.

Officer Pat shrugged. "Anytime there's rumors of pirates associated with a place, you can bet there's stories of hidden gold. Locals don't take such nonsense seriously, but maybe a visiting youngster or two with a bent for mean shenanigans decided to check it out. I'll go back to the office and get the lowdown on who's new around here. Well, besides you two."

Janice looked up at Shane. "When you visited here as a youngster, did you hear tales of pirate treasure associated with Moran Cottage?"

The question set Shane's teeth on edge, but he forced a smile. It wouldn't do to let Officer Pat see he was uncomfortable with the revelation of this piece of personal history.

"I don't remember even hearing Moran Cottage mentioned."

At least his answer brought a smidgeon of relief to the tension around Janice's lips. "If I— If *we* can bring the place up to snuff, maybe we can start hearing this place spoken about in a positive light."

Officer Pat let out an affirmative hum. "That would be nice. Even nicer if the place were inhabited so the department doesn't have to keep dispatching officers to check out imaginary, or in this case, real disturbances." She tucked her nightstick into her belt. "I'd better get back to the station with my goodies. Oh, am I going to have a great time razzing some of the guys who half bought into the spook stories."

The officer walked away, chuckling.

Janice stared at Shane. Shane stared back.

"What?" she said. "You're not happy with the flesh-and-blood explanation?"

"We're dealing with genuine twenty-first-century human beings all right, but… Oh, never mind. I'm probably not remembering right."

He turned to walk away, but Janice grabbed his arm. Her fingers were slender, graceful and stronger than they looked.

"Don't keep things from me. Even if it's only something you suspect. I despise being treated like I can't handle the full picture."

Shane dropped his gaze. Way to sucker punch him.

He drew in a deep breath and reengaged her steady look. "I was in the basement yesterday and I noted not one but two egress windows blocked by overgrowth. The openings were recessed and small enough that I didn't take them seriously as access points for an intruder."

"Did the windows have intact panes at that time?"

"That's just it." Shane spread his hands. "I'd like to think I would have noticed if a pane was missing, but the lighting situation down there is terrible, especially with those windows blocked. One thing I do know, I didn't find any broken glass on the floor as one might expect if an intruder had shattered a window to get inside."

"So someone cleaned up after himself after he broke in and fiddled with my step? That makes no sense."

"Not if the culprits were reckless teenagers."

Janice drooped. "You are so right. I seem to be in the crosshairs of a mature and determined malice. Or maybe not me so much as anyone taking an interest in this place."

Shane suppressed a shudder at her use of the term *crosshairs*. She had no idea how accurate she might be if the Morans were behind the sabotage and decided to escalate their attempts to get her to leave.

Janice pressed a hand to her forehead. "I need to fire you, Shane." She stared up at him. "You need to get away from here as fast as you can. I can't take responsibility for—"

Shane gripped her shoulder with one hand and placed a finger across her lips with the other. "If you're not leaving, I'm not leaving."

"Why?"

He opened his mouth, closed it, swallowed then expelled a long breath. "Would you believe me if I told you I'd never forgive myself if one more bad thing happened to you that I could have prevented?"

Gradually her shoulder relaxed beneath his hand, and she smiled. Alarm bells jangled in his gut.

How was she taking his statement? As a declaration of personal feeling? That assessment was too close to accurate for comfort, but better than having her guess he had an ulterior motive for interest in the cottage. Blast those Morans! Right when he meets the most fascinating woman of his life, he has to be playing cat and mouse with the mob.

EIGHT

"Here's the shattered glass." Janice pointed her flashlight beam into a corner of the cellar that had lain in darkness beyond the reach of the glow from a pair of lightbulbs hung at opposite ends of the ceiling. The pile of broken shards glinted back at her.

"Someone swept them into the corner." Beside her, Shane planted his hands on his hips. "I wonder why."

She gazed around at the earthen floor. "Someone seems to have swept the entire basement with a broom. See the marks of bristles in the dirt?"

"Now that you mention it…" Shane frowned.

"But again we have to ask why. A treasure-hunter with an obsessive-compulsive neatness disorder?"

Shane spurted a laugh then sobered. "I'm so baffled it isn't funny."

"I agree with you there."

Shane squatted for a closer look. "Actually, I think these marks were made with a rake. The kind you use on a yard full of leaves in the fall."

"Maybe whoever did this was trying to mask some illicit excavation down here." Janice hugged herself.

Possibly the intruder hadn't tried to unearth something hidden, but had buried something he hadn't wanted to be found. Horror stories of bodies stashed in basements hit too close to home—smacked of serial killers or even contract killers disposing of their victims. She shoved the awful thought away. Janice hadn't looked at those mental snapshots in years and she wasn't about to start now. Once triggered, her dreams about that nightmare time in her early adulthood were worse than the more recent horrors from Denver.

A touch on her arm drew Janice back to herself. Shane was staring at her closely. She tried on a smile for his benefit.

"Sorry about that. I must have been engaged in the same sort of woolgathering you were doing on the porch."

"No worries, Tuff. Let's poke around. See if there's a soft spot in the floor down here."

"Right."

Janice inhaled a deep breath and joined Shane in hunting for a telltale patch of loose dirt, the feel of give beneath her feet or the sound of something hollow below if she stomped hard. They came up with nothing. The floor was as solid as the next thing to rock.

"Let's take a look in the shed out back," Shane suggested. "Maybe they got their rake from there."

"But the shed's locked."

"Humor me. I've still got my reservations about the idea someone broke in through the cellar window. If they picked the lock on the front door, for instance, the lock on the shed wouldn't have stopped them."

"Have it your way." She threw up her hands.

They trooped out to the backyard, and Janice inserted one of her keys into the rusty lock. It resisted turning. "See?" she said, stepping back to allow Shane a shot at it with his two good hands. "It's practically rusted solid. Nobody's been picking this lock."

"Okay, I was wrong, but let's check out what's in here anyway." The key turned with a grumbly snap and Shane pulled open the protesting door.

Scents of must and old grease and gasoline residue spilled out. They peered inside together.

"Whew!" Janice waved a hand in front of her face. "Any gasoline in that old push lawn mower must have evaporated."

"Junk city! There's so much stuff piled in here it makes the place look dinky."

Janice groaned. "We'll have to tackle the cleanup one of these days, but the chore is somewhere near the bottom of my list."

"We could use this right now though." Shane picked up an object leaning on a jumble of twisted metal.

"An ax? I'm sure it's dull as a hammer."

"Maybe not. The head's been wrapped in oilcloth." He pulled the cloth off and exposed gleaming metal.

"What are you planning to chop?"

"I'm going to take a whack at the rusty chain holding the outside cellar doors shut. If we can open those wide, a lot of light would spill into the cellar. Maybe we'll notice something we haven't before."

"I guess this trip to the shed wasn't a waste of time, after all," she said as she followed Shane to the cellar doors.

His shoulder and back muscles rolled as he brought the ax down on the thick chain. Janice scolded herself sternly for noticing and admiring. He chopped once. Then again. Then a third time and the chain sprang free. Shane yanked at the door handles.

He shook his head. "It's latched on the inside."

"One way to fix that." She motioned him to follow her, and they went back down into the cellar from the inside.

Janice climbed the thick cement steps that led to the outside doors. The inner latch was just that, a burly hook that proved fairly easy to dislodge. She backed off onto the floor of the cellar and let Shane shoulder the double doors open and fling them wide. Brilliant sunlight streamed onto her face, and fresh air blew into a space that had moldered in the dark for decades.

Eyes open wide, arms spread, Janice turned around and around. Then she let her arms flop to her sides. "This space is pretty hopeless."

"What do you mean by that?"

"I was considering trying to transform it into another living area, but even with the outside doors open, the light only reaches a few yards in any direction. If I pour concrete over this floor, it'll still be a dank, dark dungeon."

Shane tapped a finger to his chin. "Might be a perfect man cave."

Janice barked a chuckle. "I'll grant you the cave part."

"I wouldn't give up on the idea of cementing this floor. Should bring the value of the place up, even if the cellar becomes only storage space or an emergency hurricane shelter for the new occupants."

"Thanks for the encouragement, but I'm already tired of this place for one day. I have errands to run in town, not least of which is to pick up a landline phone so we have something to connect to the outlet when it goes live. Will you be okay hanging out here finishing that porch? I'll bring us back something delicious for supper. I promise."

"Sounds like a deal to me."

Were his words too eager, his smile too bright? Unsettled, Janice led the way up the steep stairs into the hallway above.

"I'm going to rent a residential grade buffer," she said, pointing toward the scuffed and dull but original wood flooring. "Once we get the floors buffed and refinished, we can start bringing in furniture from the storage unit. Get the place modestly livable until the rest of the work can be done."

"Buffing and waxing tomorrow then."

"Probably over the course of the next full week." She scrunched up her nose as they walked into the front sitting room. "We'll be lucky to get through one room a day. I warn you, I'm going to be a stickler for perfection."

"We should probably have the chimney cleaned before you buff and wax in here." Shane gestured toward the mammoth fireplace.

"Good call. You don't have a side gig as a chimney sweep, do you?"

"Bring me the right equipment and I'll see what I can do."

"I was joking."

"I'm not. And since we've found the right tool for it already, I'll even chop wood for our first evening blaze."

Janice's face warmed. That idea sounded dangerously cozy. Good thing he couldn't see her discomfort. He was striding toward the hearth.

"Ever made s'mores in the house?"

"I'll add the fixings to my list," she said and headed toward the kitchen.

The image of herself snuggled up against Shane in front of a crackling blaze chased her out the side door. An ocean breeze blew the nonsense out of her brain.

Stick to business, girlfriend. Romance is a four-letter word to you right now.

On the drive toward Edgartown, Janice tuned the radio in to an all-music/no-news station. News reports of any sort gave her anxiety. A phobia too weird to allow many people in on the personal quirk. Shane would think her psycho for sure. But from the day her world blew up and she lost her parents, she'd been unable to get past the irrational fear, so she avoided television altogether and indulged in highly selective radio listening.

The Christian pop hits soothed her, and soon she was singing along with the music to quiet the voice of conscience. At the top of her list of errands, she had deliberately failed to mention to Shane a stop at the town library. Not that it was such a big secret that she'd decided to research the history of Moran Cottage. He'd probably agree with that endeavor in case the information shed light on current shenanigans. But she also planned to log into a computer at the library and check out that web address she'd found under Shane's laptop.

An hour and a half later she emerged from the spanking-new and very complete Edgartown library, good arm laden with a couple of thick tomes on Martha's Vineyard history and pocketbook lightened by ten dollars. Since she didn't care to claim ownership of Moran Cottage, she had to fork over the nonresident fee for a library card. Small price to pay.

Reading the website article from the online Buffalo, New York, newspaper had given her the shivers. It was a recent follow-up to an old scandal related to the death of Reggie Moran, the prior owner of the Martha's Vineyard cottage. Reggie was an uncle several times removed whom Janice had never met. Though the man's death had occurred almost two years ago, authorities hadn't notified her of the bequest until they'd resolved pending criminal complications. Then they'd cleared the title for release to the heir. She still couldn't fathom why Reggie had left the place to her, unless it was some feeble attempt at making up for the lie the first eighteen years of her life had been.

Some bequest! So far, the place had nearly gotten her killed a time or two.

But why was Shane interested in the blurb about the crash of a small plane that cost the pilot and only occupant his life? The article said that, following lengthy investigation, pilot error was the cause of the accident. The story went on to briefly recap the raid on Reggie Moran's air-freight business following his death. Several of Reggie's employees had gone to prison for complicity in transporting stolen goods, racketeering and blackmail. A diversity of criminal enterprises that surprised Janice not at all.

When the crash occurred, Reggie had been flying in a direction contrary to his logged flight plan. Fleeing the FBI raid he'd caught wind was coming or had there been another crook after him for rumored double-dealing? Media had speculated about both possibilities, even of foul play in his death. But apparently the authorities had closed the book on the case, satisfied with the malefactors they'd bagged.

If Reggie Moran had been murdered, he certainly hadn't been afforded justice. A part of Janice was tempted to call it reaping what he sowed and leave it at that, but the standard of justice was the same for anyone, the known crooks and those who managed to live on the right side of civil laws but violated God's laws all the time. Truth be told, by Divine standards everybody deserved death, but the same standards decreed that nobody deserved to be murdered.

Janice shook her head as she stowed her treasures in the car. Fine time to wax philosophical—and about injustice to a Moran at that. While she deeply despised her heritage, she intensely prized the mercy and grace that she of the Moran lineage had received as a free gift in Jesus Christ. The Lord made her whole and kept her sane. He'd do the same for anyone.

She got behind the wheel and started the vehicle. What was Shane's interest in the article about Reggie Moran? It didn't make sense to believe Shane was researching *her*. He didn't know she was related to the former owner of the cottage. Of course, he might be researching the cottage itself. To what end? Did he have designs on the place he hadn't made known to her? Of course, the reason for the research could be entirely innocent. Idle curiosity even.

She'd see how he reacted to the books she was bringing home. Excessively interested? Uninterested? Either response would aggravate her insecurities where Shane Gillum was concerned. Was he a gift horse or a Trojan horse?

Laying aside her misgivings for the moment, Janice

pursued other errands and soon had her vehicle stuffed full of buffing equipment and supplies, chimney-cleaning equipment and instructions, as well as the library books, a telephone and a few groceries. Her arm was starting to ache—her whole body, actually—and she donned her sling.

One more stop to make, other than to pick up a pizza at a place recommended by the librarian. The GPS on her phone, which was thankfully operational in Edgartown, showed the location of the storage unit in the airport industrial park. She drove there with minimal problems, but getting the assistant manager to let her into the interior of the main building was another story.

Finally, after he looked up the letter she'd had her attorney send ahead, granting one Janice Swenson owner's agent privileges, he unlocked the facility and escorted her toward the pair of 10' x 20' units required to house all the furnishings and bric-a-brac from the cottage. In foresight not untypical of Moran attention to detail, Uncle Reggie had purchased a long-term lease for the storage. That lease, the assistant manager did not hesitate to inform her, would run out in another month. Janice took the news with a noncommittal nod, but silently challenged herself to dispose of the contents within that time frame.

The interior of the warehouse-like building was cool, but not cold, and smelled of metal and cement. Their footsteps echoed in the hallway that sliced between successions of garage-style doors, which appeared to extend into infinity.

"The Moran Cottage units haven't been visited since we opened for business in 2003, and the material was transferred from a defunct facility." The middle-aged manager shot her a speculative look. "The contents could be quite aged. Of course, our climate-controlled environment will have preserved articles as intact as they were received."

Janice just smiled. The guy was covering his bases should she find moldy, mildewed or damaged items.

"The antiquities should make for interesting browsing," she said. *And I'll bet you'd like a look yourself.*

She stood in front of the first unit, twiddling the key between her fingers, until the guy strode off up the hallway. Then she turned and inserted the key into the lock. Smooth fit. Inhaling a deep breath, she pressed a button and the door slid upward as if greased.

Janice flicked on the light and stared at a jumble of stacked furnishings, many of them sporting nineteenth-century details such as brocaded upholstery or round, tapered Louis XVI legs and oval chair backs. Stacks of common cardboard boxes contrasted with the vintage furniture. Here and there she even spotted some pressboard furnishings from the eighties. Those would never be antiques. Curiosities maybe, but not collectibles.

She might be wise to rent a Dumpster, and she'd definitely require Shane's help in going through this stuff. But today she wanted to eyeball in privacy what she was up against. Perhaps she'd actually been the slightest bit skittish about what might lurk behind these closed and locked storage doors.

Janice went to the next unit and opened it. More of the same. At least nothing was obviously amiss in either container. A narrow aisle led between the stacks of furnishings and boxes. She wandered down it. Her lone footprints in the dust were clear indications that she was the first visitor here in a good long time.

An ornately carved ormolu desk perched atop a stack of other furnishings caught her eye. Very feminine. Too bad she'd already decided to unload the whole works. She reached up to rub one of the legs, which was just above her head. The years of vibrations from jets passing overhead must have shifted the stack enough that the desk was sitting precariously because it suddenly tumbled sideways and crashed down onto whatever was on the other side.

At the sickening snap of breaking wood, Janice sucked in a gasp. She hurried up the aisle and stared at the damage. The heavy desk had landed, legs-up, atop a pile of boxes that had burst open and scattered around it. A few wooden articles must have been in the boxes, because pieces of pressed board poked out. Most of the wood-snapping had come from the annihilation of those items, but bits of the ormolu molding on the desk had chipped and something like a miniature trap door on the underside had popped open. A weathered and slightly mold-stained book peeked out the opening.

Tiny spider feet scurried up her spine as Janice stared at the book. The cover was plain brown leather and incised on the front with letters that might once have been red but were now a faded pink.

Diary, it said.

Whose? A Moran ancestor's, of course. What horrors might the book hold? She didn't want to know…but she *had* to know.

As if she watched herself from a distance, Janice saw her hand reach out and grasp the volume. The leather was soft—worn with handling. A narrow leather strap that buckled in the front bound the covers shut just beneath the letters of the title. The buckle was stubborn in releasing but she managed to undo it. Then she gingerly peeled back the front cover.

Feminine script, faded but legible, proclaimed:

Diary of Justine Henrietta Moran, begun on the Fifteenth Day of March in the Year of our Lord Eighteen Hundred and Eighty-Three.

Janice hissed in a breath. The book she held was more than a hundred years old. The pages were thin and fragile, but she needed to read what this female ancestor had to say for herself. Heart pattering in her chest, she carefully peeled back the first leaf and began to read.

Dear Diary,
I have gradually been forced to suspect that my father is engaged in activities that neither the law nor the church would condone. Activities which, if exposed, would surely lead to humiliation, arrest and imprisonment...or even the gallows! How horrible it is to entertain such notions about dear Papa, but what else am I to think?

Have I been senselessly asleep these sixteen years of my life and am waking now into a nightmare? Has my world of respectability and affluence been built on the broken lives of others and the blood of innocents? I can hardly bear the thought, yet I must face the truth.

A sob broke from Janice's chest and she sank onto the chill of the cement floor. Had a soul sister just reached out to her from the nineteenth century?

Shane sat on the second-to-the-bottom cellar step and scowled into the bleak space. He'd finished the porch, and Janice still hadn't returned. The opportunity to have another go at the basement mystery was too much to resist, but a redoubled search across the floor produced no results except dusty tennis shoes. If the intruder hadn't been digging, what had he been doing down here that required raking the floor?

Shane's gaze scanned the walls and halted on a stone several feet up the east side—the wall that faced the ocean. If his eyes weren't playing tricks on him, the mortar around that stone was significantly fresher than the rest of the mortar around the others. What if the raking had had nothing to do with digging into the floor, but with cleaning up debris from gouging at the wall?

The leap of Shane's heart communicated to his feet. He jumped up and peered closely at the paler mortar then poked at it with a screwdriver he'd had in his back pocket from the porch work. The mortar had been in place long enough to become set and solid. Older mortar around other stones was brittle and chipped easily. Debris rained down on his toes as he jabbed at it.

Maybe the fresh mortar wasn't a sign of an intruder's search for something but of his hiding something. An electric charge zapped down Shane's spine. Could his search be about to end?

Shane began pecking away in earnest on the fresh mortar, but progress was painstakingly slow. He'd never finish digging out this stone before Janice returned. If he was about to unearth what he was looking for, he didn't want her present. For her own safety, she needed to be completely uninvolved in bringing down a sizable chunk of the Moran crime family. He had to find what he'd come for on his own and disappear from her life before returning to the risky existence of Seth Grange and delivering the goods—but not to his father. Shane didn't agree with taking the risk of that extra step in regard to precious evidence. No, he had a cop friend in New York he knew he could trust. Dad would thank him later for taking the direct route.

Shane needed to get his hands on better tools for the mortar job, such as a hammer and a chisel. And it would be nice to have a stronger source of light down here. Too much of this space was buried in shadows.

He went upstairs to the kitchen and washed his hands. The telltale crunch of tires on gravel said Janice was back. She wafted through the door on a breeze of savory scents from the pizza box in her hand. Atlas trotted close at her heels, licking his chops.

"Sorry, buddy." Shane laughed. "Pizza is not dog food."

"Aw, come on." Janice grinned. "A smidgeon of cheese won't hurt him."

She deposited the large box on the counter and Shane joined her there, sucking in whiffs of savory sauce and some kind of meat. Definitely meat. He reached for the box and she planted her hand atop the lid.

Her smile teased. "Do you want to help me unload the car before or after we dig in?"

Shane's stomach let out an audible gurgle. "My middle says after."

"Fair enough." She withdrew her hand.

He lifted the lid. "Wow!"

"Meatlovers with a twist."

"What might the twist be?" He narrowed his gaze on Janice's twinkling eyes.

"Smoked oysters. The restaurant manager recommended sprinkling a few of those in with the pepperoni, sausage and ham."

"If you had said anchovies, I'd have been out of here, but I'm game to try the oysters."

"Great!" Her grin held a hint of relief. "On the drive back here, I started to feel nervous that I might have made a mistake. I didn't want you to go home hungry after all the work you put in today. The porch looks wonderful. I'm so glad that hazard's eliminated."

Shane hefted a slice of the thickly laden pizza. "I plan to repair that cellar step tomorrow. Should be a quick project. We'll have to pick up a few replacement tiles for the roof to repair the damage up there. Might be a good idea to take care of that before the next rain or the runoff will slop all over the new porch. That should about finish the sabotage repairs, unless—God forbid—we find something else—"

"Oh, no!" Janice's eye went wide and a slice of pizza froze halfway to her mouth.

Shane's chest squeezed. "What? You found something more?"

"Not that." She set down her pizza slice on the box. "I just remembered another incident the same day as the cellar step and the roof tile. Got a few bruises out of the deal, but the whole thing seemed so minor that I forgot it."

"What minor incident?"

"Follow me." She led the way through a door off the kitchen into a sizable walk-in pantry and flicked on a light. "That." She pointed to a spot about eye height for Shane where a ripped screw hole gaped and a shelf board hung askew. About a dozen food cans bearing faded labels strewed the floor. "I walked in here, and it was a little dark because there are no windows. The top of my head grazed that shelf and *bam!* The board let loose and canned goods hammered my shoulder. Any reason to think this was due to tampering?"

Frowning, Shane looked closely at the rent drywall where the top of the shelf bracket had pulled out. The bracket dangled from its bottom nail, which had come out a few millimeters from the wall. That end of the board had come to rest on the shelf below it, which was thankfully empty and appeared sturdier than its upper-tier counterpart.

"I suppose it's possible the shelf screws were deliberately loosened, but it's just as possible that the original installer missed hitting the stud with the top screw, and time and the weight of the cans made it susceptible to falling if it was bumped."

Janice nodded and heaved an audible breath. "I'd just as soon have one less act of sabotage preying on my mind. This mess—" she motioned toward the shelf and the cans on the floor "—can wait until we're ready to paint the area, which won't be for quite a while."

"All righty then." Shane followed her back into the kitchen. "After I fix the step in the morning, we can move on to the buffing project in preparation for the furniture."

"The furniture? Yes, I—" Something flickered in Janice's eyes and then she ducked her head as she reached for her pizza slice. "I'd appreciate your help sorting through things and staging the cottage."

Why had the woman suddenly winced? She turned away, chomping a big bite, and Shane swallowed his question. Prying into whatever secrets Janice might be keeping could risk exposing his own. He'd let her preserve her privacy, as long as whatever she was holding inside had nothing to do with what he was protecting her from. And how could it, anyway?

Shane closed his eyes. His bite of pizza turned to paper in his mouth. This keeping secrets business was a tasteless affair. The whole mess couldn't be wrapped up soon enough for him. If only that didn't mean he'd never see Janice again.

NINE

"Goodbye," Janice called from the door of Shane's cabin. "See you in the morning."

Shane turned and waved. Atlas let out a deep bark then followed his master down the path toward the beach that would take them to Moran Cottage.

Janice shut the door and leaned her back against it with a sharp sigh. Finally!

Not that her evening of pizza with Shane hadn't been pleasant. He was good company. Funny. Easygoing. Diligent and then some!

When they had plugged in her newly purchased cordless phone they discovered her internet connection and phone line were live. Shane had taken his laptop with him tonight, intent on boning up on chimney cleaning so he could undertake the dirty deed personally. Plus, he'd appropriated one of those library books on island history and was going to help her scour the resources for information on Moran Cottage. He'd seemed completely casual in his willingness to help with the reading, providing no fuel for her suspicions about why he'd been looking up stuff about the Morans on the internet.

Janice's reluctant foray into research on her family and their island property might help her short-circuit or circumnavigate issues in regard to unloading the place. She'd be on that project like a flea on Atlas if not for the discovery of the diary. Reading that private and intimate record of the Morans who must have been among the first to own the cottage took precedence over practically everything else in her life. The mere thought of her discovery sent her heart rate into a skid.

She'd come within half a breath of blurting out to Shane the news of her amazing find, but—almost literally—bit her tongue to keep mum. If only there wasn't so much about her early life that no one could know. She hadn't even told her best friend in Denver more than the barest generalities. Without betraying more than she could afford about herself, how could she possibly explain to this new acquaintance her feeling of sisterhood with a young woman suddenly recognizing her family's criminal involvements?

Questions consumed Janice. How did Justine handle the revelation? What had become of the young woman? Would those answers provide valuable insights—perhaps even a measure of healing? Against her better judgment, Janice allowed a strange hope to flame into life within her.

She went to the paper sack of items she'd brought from the cottage and rummaged inside. Her fingers passed over the spine of the library book she'd kept for herself. Where was the diary? Surely she hadn't left it behind where Shane could—ah, there it was. Tension along the back of her neck relaxed as her hand closed around thickness wrapped in a scrap of oilcloth she'd found in the storage unit.

Unfortunately, because of her bum arm, she'd had to leave the beautiful desk upside-down, the way it had landed. When she and Shane went in to sort through the items, he could deal with setting it upright. Hopefully, the piece wasn't damaged beyond restoration. That antique desk was a valuable item, but what she drew from the twenty-first-century grocery sack was priceless.

God, did You arrange for me to find this?

Tenderly, Janice carried the wrapped book to the bedroom and set the packet on the bedside table. As soon as she'd showered and crawled between the covers, reading more of Justine's words would be her reward at the end of a long, busy day.

Janice relished the hot spray on her tired muscles, but made her shower quick. It was an annoyance to have to wear a plastic bag over the cast on her left arm. Thankfully, the thin cut on her scalp no longer needed to be covered and was apparently healing nicely because it hardly gave her a twinge as she shampooed her hair.

Stepping out of the windowless bathroom in comfy pajamas, Janice reached behind her to click off the light. The cabin was instantly plunged into gloom. Apparently the sun had dipped below the horizon within that short amount of time and she hadn't thought to leave a light glowing in the bedroom.

As she padded up the hallway in soft slippers, a sound stopped her cold. Was that a groan? Where had it come from—inside or outside?

The sound came again. Janice's breath caught and her heart pattered against her ribs. Definitely a groan, but from outside. Did it come from a human throat? Something about the noise wasn't right.

She caught her lower lip between her teeth. Maybe she should call Shane.

"Don't get the willies so easily, Janice," she whispered to herself.

The explanation could be as simple as a couple of tree limbs rubbing together in the yard. Shane's rental cabin was somewhat woods-enclosed, quite the opposite of Janice's exposed property.

Inhaling and then slowly exhaling, she commanded her feet to move toward the kitchen, where Shane had showed her a flashlight was kept and she could pick up the handset to the cordless phone. Armed with the flashlight in her stronger hand and the phone in her weaker, she moved from window to window, peering into the gloom.

If someone was out there, no way was she going to click on an overhead light or the flashlight—not yet, anyway—and pinpoint to some intruder her location in the house. If it turned out the sound was human and the person needed help, she would have time enough to produce light and punch in 9-1-1 or call Shane. If the sound had a natural explanation, she could put the flashlight and phone away, start breathing normally again, and go about her evening's business. A lot of ifs, but she prayed the situation was the latter and that she was creeping around in the dark for no reason.

So far, so good. She'd peeped out the window in the front door and the one over the kitchen sink. Also the one on the south side of the living room. By the vigorous wave of tree branches, the wind must be kicking up from the Atlantic. A brine tang salted the air inside the cabin.

As Janice proceeded to the other side of the living room, the fabric of her pajama pants shushed against a thickly upholstered ottoman that was barely visible in the self-enforced gloom. At the contact, a tiny shiver flowed up her body. She reached the set of heavy drapes that covered the large rectangular panes of the north window and stopped. Janice held herself still and listened. The odd, eerie sound had not repeated itself since she'd begun hunting for its source.

Inside the cabin, silence thickened. Outside, the high-pitched *whoo-whoo* of the wind in the eaves resembled not at all the low moan that had sent her on this spook-hunt. Not that she believed in spooks, but she was beginning to feel as foolish as someone who did.

With her flashlight, Janice parted the curtains and peered out. Nothing. Not a—

A guttural moan sliced the darkness, jabbing Janice's pulse rate into a wild gallop. The sound had come from right outside this window!

Sickly green brilliance erupted and a face—skin blue-white and slack like a drowned person's—plastered itself against the windowpane. The eyes glowed. Not the way a cat's eyes reflected moonlight, but as if the creature was lit from within. Phosphorescent seaweed draped the scalp and the mouth yawned wide and as dark as a bottomless pit.

A soundless cry gagged Janice as the thing's tortured moan lengthened and deepened. She stumbled backward. The ottoman caught the backs of her legs, sending her into a tumble, end over end. Pain fizzed up her right arm as her funny bone smacked the hardwood floor.

She lay flat. Sprawled. A scream at last burst from her chest. Ignoring the pain of her fall, she scrambled onto her knees. The face was gone, the moan had stopped, but her heart pursued its attempt to claw out of her chest.

The phone! Where was it?

That lifeline to sanity had flown from her fingers. Whimpering and snuffling, she groped about on the floor and finally found the handset. Her fingers froze over the keys. Nine-one-one or Shane? Of course, she knew she should call the emergency number but how long might it take for help to arrive at this remote location? Shane could race over in minutes. If only she could remember her new number.

"What is it? What is it?" The question streamed between her lips as her brain fought for coherent thought. Then the digits flowed into her consciousness. She'd repeated them to herself during the hike from her place to his this evening.

She stabbed the keys with shaking fingers. The phone rang…and rang…and rang…and—

"Hello?"

Why did Shane sound out of breath? Never mind!

"Come quickly! Someone… Something is outside the cabin. It was just at the window. Come!"

"Hang tight! Atlas and I are on our way."

Tears burned behind Janice's eyelids as the line went dead. If the creature was still moaning, she couldn't hear the sound over the roar of her pulse in her ears.

"I believe you, honey. Of course, I do." Shane squeezed Janice closer as she trembled against him in the brightly illuminated kitchen of his cabin.

Had she noticed the endearment that had slipped out? What was he doing getting this close to her? What else *could* he do but hold her? Her head rested on his shoulder right where he wanted it. What a disaster for his sanity that she felt so soft and perfect in his arms.

"But the story sounds so ridiculous…so unbelievable coming out of my mouth."

She lifted her head and backed away a step. Atlas whined, sniffing at the legs of the woman he seemed to have adopted as his mistress. Shane commanded his arms to fall to his sides. He needed to get a handle on this urge to wrap them around her again.

"If you say you saw something, you did, and you have every right to be skittish about strange noises. Now Atlas and I are going to scout around outside and see what it might be."

"O-Okay. Don't take any chances."

Her voice trembled and Shane's hands fisted. What he wouldn't like to do to whatever culprit had terrified this brave woman so badly!

"While we're gone, why don't you heat water for tea? I think there's some lemon chamomile somewhere in the cupboards."

An unsteady giggle passed between her lips. "Somehow you didn't strike me as a tea guy."

Shane forced a grin. "Healthier alternative than a shot of whiskey after a stressful day in the ambulance."

"You got that right." Janice squatted and with both hands ruffled the fur around Atlas's neck. "Go get 'em, boy. I think the bogeyman has left the grounds, but maybe you can sniff out some clue about what's going on." The dog rumbled a brief woof.

Shane hefted the flashlight and called Atlas to follow. The dog practically pushed him over in an attempt to squeeze past his master out the door. An abnormal intensity seemed to have supplanted Atlas's laid-back nature.

The animal proceeded directly around the corner of the cabin and beelined for the window where Janice said she'd seen the eerie face. Atlas poked his nose into the turf below the sill, sniffing intently. Shane directed the flashlight beam onto that area of the ground. No evidence of the…whatever-it-was showed in the grass, but his dog definitely smelled something not kosher. Shane scanned the light slowly over the entire area—grass, trees, window, wall and even the sky. He could see nothing, at least not in the dark. He'd have to look again in the morning.

Shane heaved a long breath. What to do now? If shenanigans were going on at his place, it seemed a foregone conclusion that the target was Janice personally, not some creep trying to scare off whoever came to Moran Cottage. Who was Janice Swenson that she'd draw this type of attention?

He needed to unearth her secrets, the sooner the better, but he'd have to be careful how he went about that project. He couldn't afford to scare her off and put an end to his access to the cottage. Unless, of course, he was within minutes of finding what he'd come for. When she had called tonight, he was in the cellar finishing the process of chipping away the mortar around that suspicious stone block. He'd know the answer to that possibility as soon as he went back to the cottage. If only he felt comfortable leaving Janice alone again.

Shane reentered the cabin, Atlas trotting at his side, apparently content once more now that he'd thoroughly sniffed the violated ground. They found Janice pouring hot water from a saucepan into a pair of mismatched mugs. The mellow scent of chamomile trailed upward in the steam. Her head turned toward them as they trooped in and her green gaze shot questions.

He offered a tense smile. "Someone was definitely out there. Atlas smelled the person loud and clear."

She chuckled. "*Smelled* loud and clear?"

"You know what I mean." His face relaxed a bit. "Nothing is there now, but I'd like to take another look in the morning."

"Unless we find something tangible, I'd just as soon not report this incident to the police."

"Why?"

"I have this sneaking suspicion they'll chalk the matter up to a hysterical female on edge because of recent accidents at Moran Cottage."

"Those accidents weren't accidental, and they were real enough. The cops know that."

"Yeah, but this one smacks of those ghost stories that are rife around the island about this area of the coast. I don't want any part of contributing to such things. Or of encouraging this low-life practical joker by supplying free publicity."

"Gotcha. I can't say I disagree in principle, but I don't like the sense that you could be in danger."

"Me, either." She handed him a mug of tea. "But now that I've had a chance to calm down and think, I figure that if my sleazy prankster had wanted to hurt me, he could have done it easily. He just wanted to scare me and obviously didn't care if his antics resulted in injury." She rubbed her right elbow.

Shane set his mug on the counter and strode over to her. "Let me see."

She turned away from his reaching hands. "No lasting injury. See?" She lifted her mug. "A mere bruise on my funny bone."

"Not so funny." His jaw tightened. "What are we going to do now?"

"Drink our tea and call it a night. The adrenaline rush has left me and I'm absolutely drained."

"You actually want me to leave you alone?"

"Um, well, maybe this time I'll let you leave Atlas with me."

"Done deal."

Twenty minutes later Shane arrived at Moran Cottage slightly out of breath from hurrying. He'd left the front door unlocked in his rush to get to Janice, but he saw no sign of disturbance as he stepped through the door into the main living area. Not that there was much to disturb in this room. He peered into the kitchen and into the bedroom where he slept, but all remained as he'd left it.

The tension had ebbed from him, leaving an empty exhaustion similar to what Janice had said she'd felt. Still, he couldn't turn in before revealing whatever lay behind that stone in the cellar.

Shane hurried below as fast as the steep steps allowed. After Janice had left for the evening, he'd made a quick trip to the lumberyard where they'd bought the porch supplies and caught the Larry-Chuck worker getting ready to close the place. The guy helped him grab a chisel and a battery-powered trouble light he could hang from a hook tamped into the more brittle mortar. Not that he told Larry-Chuck what he intended to do with the supplies.

The trouble light hung faithfully aglow where he'd left it. The hammer and chisel lay undisturbed in the dirt where he'd dropped them. But the stone was tumbled out onto the floor and a dark hole gaped at him from the wall, mocking the way his efforts had benefitted someone else.

Shane sank onto a wooden step. That prank on Janice hadn't been about her at all. It was about getting him away from the cottage. Did that mean Janice was safe now? His chest swelled with an odd feeling. Relief?

Then he dropped his head into his hands as bitterness flooded his mouth. Sure, he was glad the danger was over for Janice…for him even. Why would the Morans bother going after Seth Grange if he could no longer hurt them? He could return to being himself. Return to work even. But he'd failed his father, their family name was destroyed, and the guilty had escaped unscathed.

The Morans had won. Again.

TEN

Janice struggled up the steep ascent from the beach toward the front yard of her property. It had been two weeks now since Shane and she had begun switching places at night, and she was still breathing harder from the uphill effort than she would have liked. Since her brief stint in the hospital a couple of months ago, recuperating from the attack in Denver, she hadn't found time or energy to go to the gym. Then she received notice about the inheritance and jumped at the chance to get away for a while.

Maybe she should change her mind and look into a fitness club in the area. Her arm was better. A reinforced soft cast now encased her wrist and hand with a Velcro closure. But she still didn't trust her arm strength to ride a bike, and she was precious little good to Shane in the renovation work. Then again, she could continue to settle for the exercise of long walks along the beach with Atlas. She and Shane were taking turns keeping him overnight. At least the dog was better company than Mr. Grumpy.

What had gotten into Shane? Didn't he like the cessation of funky incidents? Since the freakish scare-tactic at the window of the cabin, the past couple of weeks had gone smoothly. Well, except for the persistent delay in the arrival of those plumbing parts. Hopefully, that happy event would occur this morning when the ferry docked from the mainland.

At last Janice reached the top of the ridge and stopped to let her heart rate slow while she contemplated the cottage. Except for the new porch, the outside showed little progress for two weeks of work. Shane had kept the sparse lawn around the cottage mowed with a rented push mower, but that was about it. The clapboard siding cried out for paint, but all in good time.

At least the exterior was more presentable than the mess happening on the inside from the activities of the plumber and the electrician. Even though the power worked throughout the building, the wiring and outlets were old and needed to be brought up to current code to satisfy the type of moneyed buyer Janice wanted to attract.

Ultimately she'd had to postpone refinishing the freshly buffed floors until after the professionals were done creating dust. But Shane *had* swept the chimney and then ripped out those hideous countertops in the kitchen.

Now the two of them made their noontime sandwiches on a card table brought over from his place and ate them perched in two of a foursome of folding chairs on the new porch, watching the ceaseless movement of the ocean. Ships and boats of all sizes and shapes regularly passed beneath their viewpoint, and the gulls wheeled and squawked in the pale blue sky. The weather had been gorgeous these past weeks, except for the storm cloud that constantly shadowed Shane's expression.

Maybe he was put out that he was still sleeping on the blow-up mattress and that he had to hike over to his place every evening to take a shower then scoot back to her place for the night. It was a huge commitment, truly going above and beyond, and perhaps the arrangement was wearing thin. Yet, yesterday when she'd suggested that the shenanigans appeared to have run their course, and maybe they could drop the switcheroo, he'd nearly bitten her head off.

Sure, he'd apologized immediately for his strong reaction, but she was left once more with the sense that Shane Gillum had a hidden agenda.

Deep woofs carried to her from inside the cottage and the front door opened, releasing a giant fur ball that torpedoed toward her, tongue flapping from jaws grinning in doggy glee. Shane sauntered outside, cradling a mug and calling a warning to his enthusiastic pooch. The animal stopped just short of bowling Janice top over tail down the hillside. Atlas stood still, adoring her with his eyes and wagging his hind end nearly in circles. Janice laughed and scratched the animal behind soft, fuzzy ears.

"You missed me, eh, boy?"

Atlas was another bone of contention between her and Shane. Honestly, if she didn't know better, she'd think the guy was jealous of how much his dog seemed to love her. Then why did he so happily give his blessing every time she wanted to take Atlas out for a walk along the beach?

Was she that much in the way of progress in the cottage, or did he feel regret for holding and comforting her when she was so scared that night? He had made it abundantly clear in his actions and attitude since then that he had no personal interest in her. They shared no more suppers together. If they went to a restaurant in the evening, it was on their own. She got the picture already, so couldn't he lighten up?

If not for the nightly comfort of reading a few entries in her ancestress's diary, the rejection might hurt. More than it actually did, anyway. Shouldn't she be relieved that he was nipping in the bud any attraction they might have felt for one another?

"Hi, Camper." Janice waved at her amateur handyman.

To her great surprise, he smiled at her today, and her heart tripped over itself. She would have to schedule a stern talk with that contrary organ.

"Come on in, Loafer." He waved her onward. "The coffee is on."

She followed him into the kitchen and he poured her a steaming mug. As he handed her the coffee, he gazed somberly into her eyes from beneath those stunning lashes.

"I've been wrestling with a decision," he said. "Maybe you've been able to tell."

"Ya think?" She quirked one side of her mouth at him then slurped at the hot brew.

"I'm sorry I've been such a bear. Truly."

How did a girl stay irked with a guy who looked at her with the same big puppy-dog eyes as Atlas did when he was wordlessly apologizing for some faux pas? Well, at least she could pretend to keep the guy on probation.

"Hmm. You might be forgiven. It depends on the nature of this decision. You're not quitting on me, are you?"

"No…no, I'm not. That idea has been on the table, though, due to some things in my personal life that I didn't want to burden you with."

"It can be nice to share a burden once in a while."

"True, but this…this issue involves another besides me."

She locked gazes with him. Unless she was grossly misreading him, he was sincere as all get-out. But who was this other person? She dropped her gaze.

"A girlfriend? A fiancée? I mean, that's okay. It's only natural you'd be seeing someone, I—"

"Whoa, there, Tuff." He laughed and tugged a lock of her hair that had strayed from her ponytail. "No girlfriend, and certainly no fiancée."

"What's so funny? Any woman would count herself blessed to…"

Janice let her voice trail off. Way to start sounding pitiful. How far gone was she about this guy and hadn't even realized it? The man treated her like a kid sister, for pity's sake. She set her half-empty mug on the table and turned toward the side door.

"Thanks for the coffee. I think I'll go start sorting through what's in that shed in the backyard. I've been meaning to do that."

"Wait!"

The urgency in Shane's tone stopped her but she kept her shoulders squared and her back to him.

"My intent was the opposite of making you angry! When I finish my explanation you might be pretty annoyed, but I hope you'll also be relieved."

"Okay, let's have it." She turned, crossing her arms. "What haven't you been telling me?"

"Sit with me." He pulled out the folding chair in front of her coffee.

Janice complied, holding her tongue, and Shane sat kitty-corner from her. He fiddled with the handle of his mug then sighed.

"The person I've been protecting is…someone I care about who got into serious trouble through…ignorant association with the guy that your employer inherited this place from."

"Reggie Moran, the mobster?"

"You know about him?" Shane's eyes widened.

"It would be my business to be aware of such a thing when going in to sell a property."

"Okay. Yeah, I suppose that's true."

Janice suppressed a pang of conscience for not confessing her snooping around his laptop. That website article hadn't told her anything she hadn't known already. Or maybe the pang came because she still couldn't—no, wouldn't—tell a soul that she was more than just the seller's agent. If she ever hoped to have a life out from under the shadow of shame, the last link to her Moran heritage had to go the way of this cottage. Then no one would have to know who her parents were. Ever.

Shane leaned toward her. "This person told me that the last place Reggie visited before his death was Martha's

Vineyard." He tapped the tabletop with a fingertip. "That the mobster hid proof here that would put away quite a few Moran family members and exonerate the innocent."

"Here?" Janice's voice came out shrill and she half rose from her seat. "The proof is hidden on this property?"

Shane tugged her down with a grip on her arm. "Not anymore."

"What?" She gaped at him. "Would you please make sense?"

"When I came to the island, I hoped the place would stay abandoned and I could poke around at my leisure. Then when you showed up and scary stuff started happening, I figured you needed someone who knew what was going on to look out for trouble and watch your back."

"Watch my back? You're digging yourself in pretty deep, buster. Just what *is* going on? Are you telling me that the mobsters are also aware that this thing is hidden on the property and they've been trying to scare me off or kill me, whichever happened first?"

Shane winced. "Something like that, but I wasn't *sure*."

"And now you are? Why didn't the mob just burn down the cottage and destroy the evidence once and for all? Why didn't you go to the police and let *them* track down this *evidence?*"

He went white and tense around the lips. Janice had no sympathy. Surely, all her blood had drained to her toes by now, leaving her a vacant shell, weightless, yet anchored to her seat like a balloon tethered to an iron ring.

"I wasn't sure," he said, "because all this penny ante sabotage and pranking didn't seem like mob activity. My informant insisted the Morans were unaware of Reggie's stop-off here just prior to the plane crash. In coming to the island, I had counted on that being true. Besides I didn't know you well enough to be confident you weren't up to something yourself."

"And now you do?"

"I think so. You're a wonderful Christian woman, and I have all the respect in the world for you."

"Thanks for that much, anyway. But you didn't respect me enough to warn me someone could light a fire over my head any minute and—"

"Let me finish." Shane lifted a palm. "Even if my informant was wrong, and the mob *did* know where Reggie stashed the proof, they would never torch this place. For one thing, they couldn't be positive it was *inside* the cottage. For another, they're under the impression there's money involved in finding the documentation Reggie hid away. Big money. They wouldn't burn that."

"Under the *impression?* Money isn't involved?"

"Not according to my informant. Just a pile of evidence against mobsters the law has been after since…well, forever. And that brings me to why I didn't involve the cops. The Morans have gotten away with murder, literally, for so long because too many of the police are in the mob's pocket. More than you would believe.

"I have a friend inside the New York City P.D. I trust, but when I felt him out by suggesting that Reggie might have hidden such documentation, he scoffed. Said that lame rumor had been checked out and was a total myth. I shouldn't get my hopes up. I don't blame the guy. He's up to his neck in cases that aren't considered closed, but I think he would have taken action if I could have brought him the proof, but now…" Shane's shoulders slumped.

Janice's heart fluttered. "You've discovered this proof was a myth, after all? I'm sure that's disappointing for you. Apparently you trusted your source."

Shane shook his head. "Worse. I think the Morans found it. Snatched it right from under my nose."

She sucked in a breath and flopped back in her chair. "Why do you think that?"

"Come with me." He rose and motioned her to follow.

Mind spinning, Janice trailed him to the hatch in the hallway floor and then down into the cellar, where she hadn't ventured in more than two weeks. Since the missing window had been replaced more than a week ago, and the overgrowth chopped away, diffused sunlight spilled into the area and augmented the woefully inadequate overhead illumination. The space felt less dungeonlike and maybe not entirely hopeless, after all.

Shane led her over to a stone that seemed to be sitting loosely in the wall, all mortar missing.

Janice planted her hands on her hips. "Somebody dug a stone out of the wall? When? Don't tell me the creep sneaked in and did this while you and Atlas were sleeping upstairs."

Shane shook his head. "*I* dug the stone out of the wall. Well, almost. I noticed the mortar around this one was fresher than the rest so I decided to check it out. I'd worked the stone nearly free the night you called, frantic about the creature outside. By the time I returned from checking out that incident someone had been here. The stone was sitting on the floor, the cavity empty. I put the rock back in the hole and brooded these past two weeks about what to do. Finally, I decided I couldn't do anything but come clean with you, and if you fired me, so be it. Otherwise I'd stick around. See this job through as I promised. Either way, you'd know the danger was past and you could relax."

Her stomach lurched as if she were on a boat riding choppy water. "If you knew that, then why continue with the charade of switching domiciles every night?"

Shane made a noise suspiciously like his dog's whine. Supreme frustration?

"You'd probably need a psychiatrist to totally explain my reaction. It was as if I couldn't accept defeat just like that." He snapped his fingers. "I needed time to process that things weren't going to turn out the way I wanted. In the meantime, I've kept up the search. Just in case I'd misread the situation. Fruitlessly, of course."

He hung his head and Janice fisted her right hand to resist reaching out and soothing his crinkled brow with her fingertips.

"Then yesterday," he continued in a muted tone, "after I blew up at you, I realized I was living in denial, and that I wasn't being fair to you or to myself." Shane lifted his head and those blue eyes glinted at her. "I hate it when the bad guys win. In my line of work, the enemy is death, and I fight it for all I'm worth. Sometimes I lose, and it hurts. This…" He motioned toward the loose rock. "This hurt worse, and I won't be over it for a long time. So if you decide to keep me around, I'd just ask a little grace with my moods. I'd like to stay. I think the manual work will be therapeutic."

Janice opened her mouth then closed it again. What did she say to all this?

Her sense that Shane had ulterior motives for befriending her had turned out to be devastatingly correct. And his reasons for asking to stay apparently had no connection to any feelings for her. The pain of those realizations wrung her heart. And yet, to some extent, his motives had been compelling and his actions understandable.

If he had told her this tale up front when they'd first met, what guarantee would he have had that she would cooperate with his search? He'd probably had visions of her slapping a restraining order on him. Nor could he assume she wouldn't blab about his secret search to all and sundry. He couldn't know how much she would hate to bring that kind of attention to bear on herself or the property. Not that they had avoided much of that, given the circumstances.

At least, as he'd said, the danger was over. But some things he hadn't said. Something about this mission he'd come here to accomplish was deeply personal and intensely painful. Did she even want to know what it was?

"Leave me," Janice said, and his face drained of color. "No, I don't mean pack up and go away," she added hastily. "At least, not yet. You needed time to process. Now I need the same courtesy. Just go away and let me think." She turned her back on him and waved a hand toward the stairs.

The thud of Shane's retreating footfalls was as heavy as the pump of her pulse. Shoulders slumped, she shuffled to the cement stairs that led out of the cellar and sank onto them.

After the initial jarring notation in Justine's diary, most of what she'd been reading had turned to topics of ordinary life for a woman entering adulthood in that era—the completion of schooling, social events, young men who courted her, and Gabriel, the one in particular who piqued her interest. Then last night a lament had leaped off the page and pierced Janice's heart.

Why do I torment myself with hope for a bright future? Papa's double life could be exposed at any moment, or I may yet spend years in dread before the fateful moment strikes. When it does, and surely it must, the taint will mar anyone close to me—husband, children. I must leave Moran Cottage, flee Martha's Vineyard. Go where I am not known.

Oh, Gabriel! Gabriel! I hope your heart will not break as mine will surely shatter the moment my feet board the ferry to the mainland for the last time.

Janice stared at the loose stone in the wall. Here she was, also running from the family taint, also determined to shake the dust of Moran Cottage and all its associations from her feet, even if that meant giving up a chance at love. History certainly had a way of repeating itself.

* * *

Shane wandered up the beach, kicking random pebbles into the swishing surf. Atlas trotted from seaweed clump here to stick of driftwood there, sniffing. But even the dog's exuberance seemed muted. Only one circumstance saved this trip to Martha's Vineyard from total disaster. Janice was safe now, and thank God, she hadn't been injured worse in all this treacherous game-playing.

Would she ask him to leave? If she did, it might actually be a mercy. Being with her every day was torture. He liked her. He more than liked her, but his feelings had to remain his secret.

"Shane!"

At Janice's urgent cry, he stiffened then whirled. She tore toward him, long legs consuming the beach, silky ponytail flying behind her like a banner. What was wrong? He broke into a run and met her at a striated boulder that marked the halfway point between their two places.

"I found something!" she puffed between breaths. "I don't think your search is over."

"What are you talking about?" Shane's heart did a little kangaroo hop in his chest.

"I got curious so I went and grabbed the flashlight then dumped that rock out onto the floor again and took a good look. You're not going to believe this." She gulped in air and pressed the palm of her injured hand to her chest. "There was something way back in there, caught in a crack. I think whoever's been pranking has been trying to retrieve this stuff, not some crook's records."

She held out her fisted right hand and peeled open her fingers like a flower unfurling. Her palm cradled a thumbnail-size, clear plastic packet fat with whitish powder.

ELEVEN

Janice leaned toward Shane across the table of their booth in the Beach Shanty. "Drugs? Unbelievable!"

Her whisper drew a loud "Shh-hhh" from her supper partner. He went red around the ears and darted a sidelong glance toward other diners, who seemed perfectly oblivious. Janice grimaced and sank back against the cushioned booth seat.

Sumptuous odors of chowder, grilled flounder, cheesy mashed potatoes, steamed carrots and hot biscuits wafted to her nostrils from the variety of dishes sitting under her nose. But how could she think about eating when her mind was so full of urgent matters? A deep gurgle from her midsection answered that question. Apparently her tummy had independent ideas about what was urgent.

She ducked her head and scooped chowder into her mouth. Thick, rich goodness slid across her tongue and down her throat. Essie Mae was right to brag about this concoction. The flavor was sumptuous enough to distract a person from…well, from drugs stashed at *her* cottage!

Oh, Lord, what could happen next?

What to do now? That was probably the better question.

"What do you want to do?" Shane's soft-voiced question feathered Janice's ears like an echo of her thoughts.

"What do *you* think we should do?"

"Me?" He stabbed a thumb at his chest. "It's your cottage. Your boss's anyway. My guess is that somebody on the island has been using the abandoned place as a drop spot on a smuggling route. When you and I started poking around, we interrupted the flow. It doesn't make sense that the new owner knows anything about the operation, or he or she wouldn't have sent out a third party like you to handle renovations and sale. Maybe you should call the guy…or gal and ask what to do."

Janice wrinkled her nose. She couldn't find fault with his logic about the new owner, particularly when she knew he was spot-on, but her determination to hide her Moran roots didn't need to include faking a phone call.

"I don't think we have much choice but to report what we've found to the authorities. Just not to that particular cop." She motioned toward Officer Mitch seated across the room in civilian clothes enjoying a meal with a generous-figured woman whom she assumed was his wife.

Shane heaved a long sigh. "You're probably right, but anyone we report to is likely to call higher-ups. We could end up with DEA people ransacking the place in nothing flat."

Janice ducked her head and resumed eating. If the guy went any paler, he'd probably slide under the table in a dead faint.

That written evidence *against* the Morans and *for* his friend must be terribly important to him. And he seriously had a thing against trusting the cops. Was she buying into a tall tale about this documentation? Was Shane involved in something just as shady as anything the Morans could come up with? Maybe he was part of a rival mob!

Her heart squeezed and the bite in her mouth went sour. Why did she hate that idea so much?

Then again, if Shane was a crook, why level with her about the stone he dug out of the wall? He could have gone ahead and sealed it up again, no one the wiser. The man had been nothing but princely toward her. She wanted to trust him, yet what did she really know about Shane Gillum? He'd befriended her under false pretenses in the first place.

Well, at least he'd admitted it. She didn't have any better options but to proceed with him as her helper at the cottage. Anyone else she employed might actually be linked to the drug smugglers.

"At least now we have a logical explanation for why someone would booby-trap the place to discourage anyone from sticking around."

Shane snorted a wry chuckle. "Guess the saboteur hadn't figured on folks as mule stubborn as you and me."

"Me, for sure." She laughed and waved her empty spoon at Shane. "I'm going to call that nice Officer Pat tomorrow. Ask for her in person. What happens from there, we basically have no control over. We can only do what we need to do and let things unfold."

"Agreed." Shane jerked a nod and stabbed his fork into his flounder, but didn't lift a bite to his mouth.

Clearly his stomach wasn't as opinionated as hers. As she shoveled a bite of potatoes in her mouth, a tiny voice in the back of her mind hinted she might be eating the proverbial condemned person's last meal. A drug smuggling investigation was likely to turn up her shady heritage, as well as any number of other unsavory morsels from her past that she would just as soon remain wrapped in the napkin of forgetfulness and thrown away. Maybe Shane wouldn't have to know about her birth family, though. If she didn't dare hazard a romance with him, as much as that thought appealed, she'd at least like to walk out of his life knowing she still had his respect. In any case, she needed to keep her smiley face on.

"Cheer up, buckaroo," she said. "We'll have to trust

God that whatever agents come snooping around will be honest enough to do the right thing if they run across that whatever it is you're looking for."

He quirked a half smile at her. "When the lady is right, she's right. If anyone is trustworthy, it's got to be God."

Janice's heart lightened as mutual grins bloomed on their faces.

"It's plumb a treat to see you two enjoyin' each other's company." Essie Mae beamed down at them. "Sure glad of your business whether you come in alone or together, but food is better shared. 'Specially with that special someone."

Janice blinked up at her. For a woman as wide as she was tall, Essie Mae had a way of sneaking up on a person. Her beehive hairdo had wilted a little, probably from the heat in the kitchen, and her apron bore signs of the food she'd been serving, but her hazel eyes twinkled as if she were greeting a new day rather than nearing the end of a work shift.

"Hi, Essie Mae," Janice said. "The food is great!"

"Yeah, what she said." Shane smiled up at the waitress.

Essie Mae sniffed. "Can't tell that by how much *you've* eaten, young man." She crossed meaty arms over her ample bosom, but a smirk lifted the corners of her mouth. "Figure you're dinin' on love, lambkin." Her head turned from Shane to Janice and back again. "A blind billy goat could see the sparks flyin' between you two."

Janice's cheeks heated. Essie Mae was a determined romantic. No use bursting her bubble right now. Hopefully the woman wouldn't be too disappointed when Janice and Shane went their separate ways.

If only Janice was sure her feelings about that outcome weren't going to be far stronger than disappointment. When she gazed across the table at Shane Gillum, was she staring heartbreak in the face?

* * *

"Don't linger too long here, lambkins." Essie Mae's chins waggled with the shake of her head. "Storm comin', ayuh. It's gonna kick up somethin' fierce out there tonight."

The server waddled back toward the kitchen and Shane watched her go. Bad weather on the way? Just what they needed on top of everything else.

"We don't have to get too excited yet," Janice said. "The weather service is saying the thunderstorm is still a couple of hours away."

Shane transferred his attention to his dinner companion. She was tucking away her cell phone in her purse by her side.

"You had service?"

"For once."

"Okay. I guess we're good then." He paused and cleared his throat. "Essie Mae means well, but she sort of sees things the way she wants to see them."

He offered a smile to Janice that he meant to be apologetic for the woman's assumptions in the dating department. Did Janice get his meaning? He inferred so by the slight flush that colored her face as she nodded. Too bad he couldn't claim Essie Mae was dead wrong about his growing feelings for Janice, but he had no choice except to keep his emotions under wraps.

Janice must be wondering all sorts of things about him now that he'd confessed his ulterior motives for interest in the Moran property. Was she questioning her trust in him? How could he convey to her that he'd never, ever meant her any harm, and that he'd sincerely been doing his best to keep her safe in a precarious situation?

"I'm from New York City—Manhattan, specifically," he said.

Her eyes widened. Must be a shock to hear him spill a detail about himself.

She dabbed her mouth with her napkin. "Do you work there, also?"

"Yes. Live and work. Never been married, except to my job, much to my mother's chagrin…at least until she passed away a couple of years ago. I do regret not giving her the pleasure of grandchildren."

"Do you want children?"

"Yes. Very much."

Janice smirked at him. "It's generally a good idea to have a wife first."

Shane laughed. "Touché. I've dated off and on, but never found a woman who triggered those sparks Essie Mae was talking about *and* was cool with my unpredictable and often frenzied work schedule."

Her gaze went sober. "I'm sorry to hear about your mom. That's tough. Was she ill? An accident?"

"Both, I think." Shane sighed. "She could be a lovely person for quite a while and then *boom!* descend into a bout of depression, anxiety and paranoia. She'd been medicating the condition a long time and knew better than to combine alcohol with what she was taking, but—" He shrugged. "The housekeeper found her at the bottom of the stairs. Mom died instantly. Broke her neck. I'm glad she didn't suffer."

That was more than he could say for himself. Pain ripped a fresh hole in his insides. Could he have been more supportive of his mother over the years? He realized intellectually that anything he did or didn't do probably wouldn't have made a difference. Her psychological condition wasn't dependent on externals. But his gut didn't always listen to his head.

He'd thought he was doing his best to balance patient tolerance of her moods with the emotional boundaries he found necessary to maintain his own sanity when her paranoia kicked into high gear and she became verbally caustic and her behavior turned erratic. He'd often wondered how his dad stood the abuse. Maybe that's what kept the man's nose to the grindstone, spending extra hours on a job he didn't particularly like under the thumb of a boss he didn't particularly respect.

His father probably hadn't exhibited the healthiest response to a painful situation at home, especially considering the consequences, but that was all past. All they could do was deal with the situation as it was now. Perhaps Shane's all-consuming quest to exonerate his father had its roots in guilt about his mother. Or maybe he should pay himself a nickel for the amateur psychoanalysis.

Janice cleared her throat and Shane met her direct gaze. "As usual, when you've parceled out a little information, I feel like you're keeping the bulk of the matter to yourself."

"It's not easy for me to talk about this. Habit, I guess. Our family has hoarded a lot of dirty laundry over the years."

An odd expression stole across her face. What could he call it? Fellow feeling? Furtive hope? She opened her mouth, closed it, looked away and then returned her stare to his.

"I'm a widow."

"Sorry to hear it. Recent?"

She shook her head. "A decade ago, shortly after we moved to Denver. Sudden aneurism. Karl was the love of my life."

Shane absorbed the information like a sock in the gut. She'd already met and lost her true love. Another good reason to keep a tight rein on his romantic impulses toward this woman.

"No kids, I take it?"

"Not yet. We were thinking about it. A part of me

wishes we'd had a baby. At least I'd have a tangible legacy. But then, the child would be growing up fatherless, so I guess it's for the best." Her shrug held more sorrow than fatalism.

"You may as well know that my name has been in the news recently," she continued. "If you haven't already done it, an internet search would likely cough up the information."

"I haven't." He leaned closer, inspecting the raw hurt in her gaze. "Done the search, I mean. It never occurred to me you might be notorious." He smiled, but she didn't. Shane sobered. "Maybe I would have gotten around to it."

She nodded and laid her napkin on the table. The white paper was nearly in shreds. She must have been twisting it mercilessly in her lap. How did they get on to such painful topics in a public restaurant? Neither of them had finished the meal and it wasn't likely they would.

"You don't have to say anything more," he told her. "Should I promise not to look you up?"

Could he keep that promise? Curiosity was about to swallow him whole. And what if her reason for being newsworthy had bearing on his search at the cottage?

Janice relaxed hunched shoulders and released tension in a long huff. "No need for that. I can just tell you. A few months back I was one of the women targeted by the Raven Killer. Maybe you remember hearing about this rich guy who'd been systematically murdering members of a sorority who'd made a foolish pact when they were co-eds?"

The bottom dropped out of Shane's thought processes and his jaw flopped as if unhinged.

She lifted a forestalling hand. "Before you comment, I'll confess up front that I'm guilty as charged about participating in that pact to marry for money. Ranks up there among the dumbest things I ever did, but I was a bitter young woman at the time. No faith in God whatsoever.

However, participating in that lunatic agreement caused *me* more pain than I ever caused anyone else. Unfortunately the Raven Killer had no ability to make such distinctions… Oh, and Karl was not rich, except in love and goodness. I'd outgrown my infantile aspirations by the time I met him. Thank God!"

Shane sucked in a long breath. "You were a target of a serial killer? Wow! Yes, I remember reading about the case. The killer died, right? Trying to murder two women. One of them was you?"

She nodded and white heat rocketed through Shane's chest. If the scum wasn't already in the grave, Shane would have volunteered for the task of planting the creep there. He tamped down his feral instincts and unfurled his fisted fingers.

"Some poor jerk of a rich guy was the chief suspect for a long time before this other wealthy mogul was exposed, yes?"

Janice laughed. Her green eyes were especially beautiful when they glowed with humor. "The poor jerk you're talking about rescued us, killed the bad guy, and is set to marry my best friend in June. I'll be going back to Denver around then to act as her matron of honor. Then I plan to return to the island and complete the cottage renovations and sale…I hope. About the sale, I mean."

Shane let out a low whistle. "So you're traumatized big-time and head for the East Coast for what looks like a working vacation, but you run smack into more trouble. And you're still standing your ground? Most people would have run the other way by now. I'm lost in admiration!"

She met his compliment with a chuckle and a wave. "I may have developed a touch of claustrophobia from the deal, but now it's time for a new subject. Have you found anything in that library book I left with you that refers to pirates or smugglers connected to Moran Cottage? Or anything at all about the cottage? I need to get a handle on the place's reputation. This impending drug smuggling investigation isn't going to help that any."

Shane's face heated. "I have to ask your forgiveness. I've been kind of…distracted. I confess I haven't done much more than crack the cover and riffle the pages. That will change, beginning tonight. I promise."

He raised his palm as if swearing in front of a jury. Maybe he was. As far as he knew, the jury was still out on whether she was even going to let him stay on the project. She hadn't committed one way or the other. Her frown and sigh didn't bode well.

"I feel like I'm trapped inside a tiny room and the walls are closing in. Floor and ceiling, too. Not a good feeling for a claustrophobic."

"Pressure?"

"Ya think?" She waved a hand in front of her face with an expression like batting away a bad smell. "Kindly ignore that side trip into whine territory. If I need to forgive you, I'll have to forgive myself, too. I haven't so much as riffled the pages of the book I took to your place. Speaking of which—" she wagged a finger at him "—there is no reason for you to sleep at my place anymore. Tonight we go back to our own beds, and in the morning we compare notes on what we found in our reading assignments."

Shane's lungs expanded. "You mean I'm not banished?"

"Not yet." Her raised eyebrow teased.

"Let's blow this joint. I have some reading to do."

"To-go boxes first. I might want a midnight snack."

An hour later darkness was thickening around them as they parted company on her porch. Pebbles crunching beneath his tennis shoes, Shane headed down the path to the beach. At least the plumber had finished his work that day and now Janice had a few more modern conveniences available.

"You do nice work," she called after him and stomped on a porch board to convey her meaning.

Shane turned and waved. The woman was impossibly striking as she stood haloed in the pale nimbus of light from the picture window behind her. The freshening wind played havoc with her thick mane of hair that she had let down for their trek to the restaurant. She looked wild, free and oh-so-appealing.

"Tomorrow we start sorting through that mixed bag of treasures and junk at the storage facility in Edgartown," she said.

"Sounds like a plan." Shane dragged his thoughts back to business. "After you make a certain phone call first thing in the morning. We've delayed reporting long enough."

"Like I need a reminder."

He heard the scowl in her tone, though her face was in shadow.

"Are you sure you don't want Atlas with you?" she asked.

"Positive. He seems quite content where he's at."

The big dog sat like a statue at Janice's feet, head nearly as high as her hip.

"Okay, then. See you tomorrow."

"See you." Shane waved again and began picking his way down the incline.

Good thing his flashlight beam was strong and wide. It was a very dark night. Thick clouds masked the moon and had obliterated the stars. Wind velocity was rising. Essie Mae had been right that they were in for a storm. He sniffed the air: heavy with moisture and perhaps the metallic tang of lightning scudding toward them from beyond the horizon. Below, the sea was a roiling black mass, vast and intimidating and majestic.

No boat lights that he could see. The sailors were smart enough either to put in to harbor or well out to sea, away from possible collision with rocks or shoals. Except for some nut who couldn't be more than several hundred feet out.

Shane reached the beach and clicked off his flashlight. He stood still, searching for a repetition of the white flash he thought he'd seen. Nothing. He waited some more. Still nothing. The waves were battering the beach. Any captain who had his vessel out there so close to the beach had better skedaddle, engines full speed ahead, if he didn't want to become kindling. Shaking his head, Shane hurried toward the cabin. It would be smart to get indoors ahead of the downpour.

He'd like to think Janice and he had made progress tonight. But progress toward what? Sure, they were cracking open small doors into each other's lives, even into their private pain, but to what purpose?

He still hadn't given her his real name. How could he? No matter how he examined the issue, they had no future together. She was a strong woman who had faced down tremendous adversity. She was also pure and sweet and honest. Finding that missing evidence was becoming a distant dream to Shane, and if he couldn't succeed in proving his dad's innocence, the last thing she would want—the last thing he would want for her—was to hook up with the son of a convicted felon.

TWELVE

Janice shifted from foot to foot on the porch of the cottage while Officer Pat examined the puff-packet of white powder. Though her stomach prickled as if she'd swallowed a thistle, she schooled her breathing to remain deep and even. At least the air was light and scented with freshness. For once the perennial wind was almost nonexistent. Below the hillside, the glassy sea barely rippled.

Shane lingered near the porch railing. He was keeping a distance that suggested he was there to offer support but not to interfere. He'd had to drive over to the cottage this morning because too much driftwood and wet seaweed had scattered on the beach trail from the storm.

"We'll have to test this to be sure what it is," the officer said. "By color, texture and the type of packaging, my guess is heroin, though it could be cocaine or something else that hasn't occurred to me."

"How long will the testing take?"

"Almost no time."

"And then what?" Janice exchanged tense glances with Shane.

"We'll have to let the DEA know." Pat tucked the packet into an evidence bag. "They'll probably send someone over from the mainland."

"Someone?" Shane stepped forward. "Not a forensics crew to tear the place apart?"

"Unlikely, unless the DEA investigator finds something that suggests a deeper search is necessary. Sounds like you already located where they've been tucking the stash, and clearly the stuff is long gone. I doubt whoever is responsible will hazard using this place again."

"Hopefully, you're right." Janice didn't need a mirror to know her scowl rivaled the darkness of last night's storm clouds. "I'm out of patience with the craziness around here."

Officer Pat offered a wry smile. "I regret that your visit to our island has been so traumatic. Normally, it's pretty quiet around here."

"Quiet sounds won-der-ful."

A soft snort from Shane seconded the pronouncement.

"Here's hoping you get your wish," said Pat. "The P.D. on Martha's Vineyard is a fan of quiet, too." She waved and then got into her cruiser and drove off.

Janice quirked a brow at Shane. "Looks like we dodged a bullet on the police ransacking the premises."

"Whew!" He made a brow-mopping motion. "But I guess we're going to have to work up a little genuine sweat cleaning around here after last night's blast. You weren't kept awake were you?"

"A little," Janice confessed. "Not out of fright, but because I sometimes like to watch God's great fireworks show. It was particularly spectacular when the bolts lit up the ocean."

Shane pursed his lips and scratched his nose. "You didn't see anything out there, did you?"

"Other than wild water, you mean? Not even the seagulls cared to be loose in that storm. Why?"

"While I was on my way home, I must have imagined seeing a light flash a few hundred feet off shore only a little while before the storm hit."

"You weren't catching some sort of reflection from a nearby lighthouse, were you?"

Shane nodded. "That must have been it."

"I didn't read any of that library book the way I'd intended. You?"

"A little, but my electricity went out before I got past the first chapter. It came back on sometime during the night, but I was sleeping."

"Speaking of electricity, I hope the electrician plans to come back and finish the rewiring today."

"Don't count on it. They probably have a dozen calls due to electrical troubles from the storm."

Janice gusted a heavy sigh. "More delays."

"Yep, but that's often the way of big renovation projects. I'm going to get busy picking up debris around the property."

"And I'm going to grab some garbage bags and help you. I promise I won't try to scoop up anything heavy, but I can hold the bag while you do it."

"Let's get going then." He held out his fist and she bumped it with hers.

The action felt so right. Perfect. More than comraderie, but how could such a mundane touch actually feel... romantic?

She whirled away quickly and walked into the cottage. Whatever happened, she must remember that any association she made here must be left behind. That was the plan from the start, and she had to stick with the plan or there was no point in even being here.

The day passed in a few chores around the cottage. They also went over to Shane's cabin and picked up scattered branches from the many trees that had taken a beating in the storm. By that time, evening had come again and their plans to start on the storage units in Edgartown had to be postponed another day. True to Shane's prediction, the electrician had not showed up.

The story was different the next morning. The electrician arrived bright and early with the plumber not far behind. Impressive that the guy was making a house call to follow up on the effectiveness of his work. Janice reported everything, including the shower, was working great. The plumber left with a smile on his face and a fat check in his pocket.

On second thought, Janice figured the possibility of collecting without the delay of sending a bill in the mail was probably a strong incentive to make a follow-up house call. She didn't begrudge him, not after the lovely warm showers to which she'd been treating herself. Of course, the shower stall itself badly needed updating, but that would come in time. Surely things were going to unfold just fine from now on.

A sense bordering on euphoria clung to Janice as she climbed into the Jeep next to Shane for their at-long-last trip to Edgartown. Even the prospect of hot, sweaty work sorting through ancient furniture, knickknacks and memorabilia couldn't daunt her newfound optimism. After all, the electrician claimed he'd be done with his part by the time they got back. Then the real work at the cottage could begin. Followed by the staging for sale: the part she loved best.

"I read some last night," Shane said.

"Me, too. Martha's Vineyard has a lot of interesting history behind it. I took some of the rather grandiose hype with a grain of salt because the book read pretty much like a tourist manual. I found a few references to shipwrecks, one or two hints about pirates or bootlegging, but I didn't find anything specific to Moran Cottage."

"I did."

Janice's heart stalled. Anything said in a tone like that couldn't be good. "Tell me."

"It was only a couple of pages in the book, but the team of writers of this fairly dry history packed a lot of punch into about a dozen paragraphs."

"Cut the preamble already!"

Shane chuckled. "Patience, Tuff. Here we go, then. Back in the late 1800s there was this shipwrecking ring—"

"A *ring?*" She laughed. "You mean like a salvage company?"

"No, I mean like an organized gang of shipwreckers. They'd lure ships aground by sending false signals. Many lives were lost."

"What did the shipwreckers get out of that?"

"You were partly right about the salvaging. Here's where the Moran name is mentioned in connection with the salvage company that was later implicated in the wrecking. To Clive Moran the cottage was a summer home for him and his family and a prime spot to direct the legitimate and illegitimate aspects of his business."

"That's…that's awful!" Janice clutched her midsection.

Getting physically ill was not beyond the bounds of possibility. She'd reacted that way before when she'd been confronted with the unthinkable— No, she couldn't go there!

"Hey, are you all right?"

Shane's question jerked Janice back to awareness.

"What? Oh, yes. Maybe… Just go on with the story."

"I'm not sure I should. You were hyperventilating."

"Sorry. I seem to have a vivid imagination when someone tells me about man's inhumanity to man." She attempted a smile but succeeded only in showing quivering lips.

"I admire that. Apparently, Clive Moran's daughter, Justine, was also a sensitive soul. She—"

Aaaaagh! Did that squeal come out of her mouth or just happen in her head?

Apparently the former because Shane slid a sharp look

in her direction. "You know this part of the story? What happened?"

"No… Of course not. I—" She was protesting too much. *Stay calm, girl.* She cleared her throat. "What happened?"

"Wish I knew. The writers of the history book couldn't find out. They suspected Justine was instrumental in exposing the shipwrecking enterprise, but they found no record of what became of her after that. Rumors from that time period suggested that members of the gang, or even her own father, disposed of her before they were brought to justice. A nasty tale altogether. Clive was hung, his wife went mad and had to be confined in an asylum, and Justine vanished."

Janice closed her eyes. *Were you murdered, Justine? Is that what happened? Or did you get away just as you'd planned, even if it meant turning your back on love with Gabriel?*

Every inch of her skin itched. If she could have sprouted wings, flown out of the Jeep that second and returned to her bedroom at the cottage, she would have done it. Then again, a part of her wanted never to return to her reading. Often she dreaded turning the page for what she might find out. That's why she read only in small increments.

Now, in her mind's eye, the small leather volume smoldered beneath her pillow like a hot coal. Did she dare take it in her hands again? What if she discovered Justine hadn't gotten away? Never was able to cut the ties and have a life free of her family's taint? Would that knowledge shred the hope Janice harbored?

Shane dropped the cover on the rented garbage bin and rubbed his sweaty forehead on the shoulder of his T-shirt. At three o'clock in the afternoon the sun's power conveyed a hint of impending summer. Grasping the handles of a four-wheeled cart, he headed inside the storage building.

The climate-controlled coolness welcomed him back for another round of sorting and throwing away in the first of two storage units belonging to the Moran property.

Well, Janice did the sorting and he did the throwing. Not a half-bad arrangement if she'd take a chill pill and not act as if this was a rush job. The contents of the storage units had been moldering for two decades already. Another few days, or even weeks, weren't going to matter.

She'd been jumpy and hyper ever since he shared that story with her about the heinous nineteenth-century Moran enterprises. Granted, the tale was disturbing, but apparently no ghost stories were attached to the event that might spook prospective buyers. What should the ancient tragedy matter today to a Realtor from Denver? Unless Janice's connection to the Morans was more intimate than she'd let on. How close *was* she with this remote mystery heir?

Then again, he might simply be too ignorant of the realty business to grasp the implications. Even if he couldn't see such an obscure set of sordid circumstances affecting the sale of the place, maybe Janice looked at the matter differently. She was the professional, after all, and showed it.

Her selections of what should be set aside for furnishing and adorning the cottage, and what should be let go to Goodwill or offered to an antiques shop were crisply decisive. When he ventured to ask why, she always had sound reasoning behind her choices. She might be a slave driver, but her Realtor persona was pretty impressive.

A few of the selected items, such as some comfortable chairs and a small table had been placed in the rear of his Jeep so they would at least have a less impermanent place to relax and eat their lunches. Though they had set a number of items aside in the storage unit for staging the cottage, they wouldn't move the bulk of the furniture until the floors were ready and at least some of the painting had been done.

With all of that labor still ahead, it was probably best if they made some real headway today. He wheeled the cart through the wide-open unit door and found his work partner standing beside a jumble of upended boxes and what looked like a toppled piece of furniture as the center point of the mess. Four fancy-spindled wooden legs reached toward the ceiling.

"What happened?"

Janice jerked and looked over her shoulder at him. "I didn't hear you come back."

"Sorry." He laughed. "I didn't tippy-toe."

She sent him a strained smile, but humor didn't light her eyes as it had this morning. "Nothing *happened*. The desk was like this when we got here today."

"How do you know that?" They'd started at the front of the unit and had been steadily working inward.

A slight flush washed from her neck to her cheeks. "I was here a few days back...to sort of scan the lay of the land. When I touched this desk, something under it gave way and it upended into these boxes. I'm not sure what damage has been done to the piece, but this might be one thing I would consider keeping for myself." She turned away from him and caressed a clawed wooden foot.

What had she just said? "For yourself?"

Silence stretched several heartbeats then she let out a soft humph. "I imagine the owner would be delighted to allow me something 'in kind' for my services. The same deal would likely apply to you, if something catches your eye."

"Catches my eye?"

Janice turned toward him, brows crowding together. "Didn't you say you'd like to do some antiquing while you're on Martha's Vineyard?"

"Oh, yeah, that. I kind of got distracted from taking up a new hobby when stuff like sabotage and trips to the emergency room and discovery of illegal substances started happening. Besides, I've already fessed up to my real reason for being on the island."

She stepped closer and looked searchingly into his face. "Yes, you did. But I still think what I thought when we first met."

"What was that?"

"A lot goes on beneath the surface of Shane Gillum, and no matter how much he reveals, there is more to be known."

Shane stopped breathing. What would it be like to give this woman access to the deepest recesses of himself? His insides fluttered, but he red-lined the question and tamped down the response.

"I could say the same thing about you."

Did his voice just sound as breathy as a debutante's? He was in such deep trouble in the woman department! Maybe he should hop the next plane back to New York. But as wise as beating a hasty retreat might be for the well-being of his heart, if he didn't white-knuckle it through until he found the record of truth that would restore family honor, he wouldn't have a wholesome name to give anyone.

"Tell you what." Her grin brimmed with a resurgence of lighthearted mischief. "You help me set this desk upright so I can assess the damage and determine what restoration needs to be done, and then we'll call it quits for the day. I, for one, need a shower. Major."

"Join the grunge club." Shane laughed.

Sobering, she stepped closer to him. "I want you to know that you have my permission to continue searching Moran Cottage and grounds as much as you like."

Tears suddenly stung Shane's eyes.

"I...I..."

Janice pressed a finger to his lips. "You don't need to say a thing. In fact, unless you unearth a cask of pirate gold or some other thing of interest to the owner, I don't have to know where you're looking or what you find." She winked, turned and went to one end of the fancy upside-down desk. "Ready?" She grasped a pair of the legs.

"Are you sure you want to attempt this with your bum wrist?"

"No time like the present to test how much strength has returned."

Five minutes later, after a tussle of unearthing the antique from the mound of fallen boxes and maneuvering to make it as easy as possible on Janice's arm, they managed to set the desk upright. She stood back and surveyed the piece with a critical eye.

"A few chips and nicks that may add to its charm, but overall, not as bad as I'd feared."

From a kneeling position, where he'd ended up in the moving process, Shane added his critical eye. "There might be a problem underneath. There seems to be something hanging down. You may need a carpenter experienced in working with antique wood." He ducked his head and peered closer.

"Well, what do you know?" He snorted. "Some kind of secret drawer has popped open."

"Really?"

Janice's question hung a bit limp. He'd expected more enthusiasm.

"Anything in it?" she added almost as an afterthought.

Shane kept his head ducked, or she'd see the sudden suspicion written in bold print on his face. Had she already found whatever treasure this 8" x 8" compartment had hidden? If so, why hadn't she told him about her discovery? She'd just given him carte blanche to search for his particular "treasure." Was that move designed to blunt his desire to question her in the areas in which she continued to harbor secrets? If he didn't know that Reggie couldn't possibly have come all the way to Edgartown and entered this storage facility unnoticed to hide his documents, he'd have to wonder if Janice was somehow double-crossing him.

Surely she hadn't found something of value that she was planning to hide from the heir. No. He mentally shook his head. That idea wasn't consistent with the character she'd displayed thus far. Unless he was being masterfully fooled by a stellar actress.

He carefully blanked his expression and rose to his feet. She was already hurrying toward the exit, though the set of her back and shoulders betrayed tension.

"Hey, wait for me!" He hurried after her and arrived at her side in time to lower the garage-style door for her.

"Thanks," she said as she secured the lock.

Her smile conveyed genuine gratitude. The anger that had started to stiffen his shoulders abated. Who was he to jump to conclusions because she wasn't ready to tell him everything on her mind?

The journey back to Moran Cottage passed pleasantly enough in small talk and companionable silences. Shane rolled his head to stretch his neck muscles and contemplated a hot shower and a relaxing evening. Guiding the wheel of his Jeep one-handed, he directed the vehicle up the long approach to Janice's place.

"What in the world?" Shane burst out, and Janice gasped.

The electrician's van was gone. In its place two police cruisers and a sedan with U.S. government plates were parked willy-nilly near the cottage. A little farther away toward the descent to the beach, stood an ambulance, rear door open but no lights flashing. From the perspective of an experienced paramedic, Shane understood those details didn't bode well for whoever was involved in the emergency that had prompted the call-out.

THIRTEEN

Pen poised over notepad, Officer Mitch glowered from Janice to Shane and back again. "When was the last time either of you went down to the beachfront belonging to this property?"

Foreboding slithered through Janice's stomach. They were standing a few feet from the empty ambulance but had been allowed to come no closer. Janice stood near enough to Shane to feel his warmth, but not close enough to be touching. She processed the scene of official activity. Everybody seemed to know what was going on except her and Shane, who stood head down, hands in his jeans' pockets.

"What's going on here?" Janice asked.

"In due time." The officer's nostrils flared. "Are you going to answer my question?"

Shane shifted his stance to shoulders-back attention. "Neither of us has been to the beach since before the storm. We've used that route several times a day to walk between our places, but the storm left too much debris for easy passage, so I've driven back and forth these past couple of days. I suppose, eventually, we'd have gotten around to cleaning up down there."

The officer's pen scratched across his pad. A small flock of seagulls circled and squawked overhead. Behind them, loud barks registered Atlas's protests at being shut inside the cottage. Every sound seemed magnified by an underlying echo of tragedy. Janice suppressed a shiver.

The animal's confinement was a new development since she and Shane had departed for the day. Shane had left his dog on a long chain attached to a porch post, with food and water located in the shade of the overhanging roof.

A tall, lanky man dressed business casual, but with an official stare from piercing blue eyes strode up to them. "I'm Brady Close, chief of police. They're coming up the hill with the body now. I'll need you two to take a look and see if you know the person."

"Body?" The word squeaked from Janice's tight throat.

"I'll do it." Shane lifted a volunteering hand. "I've seen plenty of bodies in my day, but I'd just as soon spare Janice."

The chief narrowed his eyes and Mitch snorted.

"No choice involved here," Close said. "This is a murder investigation, and the body was discovered on this property, Ms. Swenson."

"Murder!" Icy fingertips slid across Janice's skin. Her arms pebbled with goose bumps, and she hugged herself. "How…? Who found the…the body?" She forced the questions between stiff lips.

"Was it the DEA agent?" Shane jerked his head toward the U.S. government vehicle.

Officer Mitch frowned with mouth tight shut, but Chief Close nodded toward the cottage. "Your dog, Mr. Gillum."

"But he was chained up."

"When Agent Durand arrived to follow up on the report of drugs found on these premises, the dog was loose and barking up a frenzy on the beach. The agent went down there to see if the animal was in distress and if he should call the humane society. The dog was standing guard over the remains, chasing scavenging gulls away."

Bitter bile choked Janice at the mental picture. And she would have to look at the body? An arm stole around her shoulder and Janice leaned into Shane's solid comfort.

A low rumble announced the appearance of a gurney at the top of the beach path, a zippered body bag its ominous cargo. A man and a woman dressed in EMT uniforms trundled the gurney toward the ambulance.

Chief Close motioned Janice and Shane to follow him. He led them on a trajectory to intercept the gurney. The EMTs halted their progress.

The chief unzipped the bag. "Do you know this person?"

Janice hung back, but Shane stepped closer. His shoulders stiffened. Janice held her breath. *Please God, not someone we know.*

"It's Moe," Shane pronounced, tone flat.

"Moe?" Janice burst out. "Who's that?"

Chief Close forestalled Shane's answer with a sharp look then directed Janice to view the body. Fists clenched, she crept nearer and looked into the pasty blue face. At least the eyes weren't open and staring, and the gulls had not attacked the facial features. The corpse looked normal except for a little bloating, the unnatural color and a round, dark hole in the middle of the forehead. No guesswork was needed to conclude foul play.

"That's one of the three workers from the Vineyard Haven lumberyard that helped demolish the old porch on the cottage. I can't recall his name, but I don't think it was Moe."

"It wasn't." Shane spoke up. "That was my mental nickname for him. Those guys were near doppelgängers for the Three Stooges. This one was Moe. I don't remember his real name, either."

"Thank you," the chief said and zipped the bag.

The noise sizzled across Janice's nerves. "May I go sit down somewhere? I'm not feeling so well."

"You can go inside, but remain available for further questions."

"I think I may know something," Shane said. "But I'm not sure it will help all that much."

Officer Mitch's pen perked up.

"Go ahead." Chief Close nodded.

"When I left here the night of the storm, shortly before the weather hit, I thought I saw a sudden flash of light out on the water. Maybe a couple hundred feet from shore. It wasn't lightning, but it could have been a muzzle flash from a discharging firearm."

"Did you hear a gunshot?"

"I didn't hear anything but thunder rumbling in the distance."

"All right. Stay on the premises until we release you."

"Will do."

Shane's hand on Janice's elbow guided her toward the cottage. At the bottom of the porch steps, he picked up the end of the snapped chain and showed it to her.

"Atlas lives up to his name in the strength department," she said.

Shane shook his head. "Amazing! Those gulls, and maybe scents we humans couldn't pick up, must have been driving him crazy."

Janice wrinkled her nose. "I hate to say it, but I thought I smelled a faint odor of rot this morning before we left. I assumed it came from all the seaweed washed up on the beach."

Inside the cottage Atlas greeted them with enthusiastic tail wags and affectionate licks on the hands that ruffled his fur.

"Good boy," Shane said as he snapped the trailing end of the broken chain loose from the dog's collar. "You don't know it, but you did a great thing by guarding that guy's body."

Janice seconded the praise and awarded Atlas extra ear scratches. Finally she met the questioning gaze Shane had fixed on her.

"You okay?" he asked. "You look pretty pale."

"I *feel* pretty pale. I think I'm officially overwhelmed. I'm tempted to leave the island. It would be so nice to regroup in a different atmosphere."

His nod was grim. "I'd be on the next ferry with you, but I doubt we'll be free to take a sabbatical from Martha's Vineyard until they've eliminated us as persons of interest."

Janice sighed. "It was just a thought. I absolutely hate the idea of being driven away from here before I've finished my job. If I gave in now, I wonder if I'd get up the gumption to come back. That would feel like…defeat."

A sharp rap sounded at the door and Shane answered it. Janice caught a glimpse of a medium-tall man, a bit on the heavy side, dressed in a sports coat and chinos. The man flipped open a badge case then slapped it shut.

"You'd be the DEA agent," Shane said and stepped aside for the agent to enter.

"Ed Durand," the man said. "I understand you discovered a packet of heroin on the property?"

Janice sank into one of the lawn chairs that remained the only seats in the house. "Shane, would you mind giving the agent the grand tour? I'll hang here with Atlas."

The dog placed his big head on her lap. Her hand automatically settled on the animal's neck and began rubbing behind his ears. Atlas's huge brown eyes drifted shut and he emitted a long doggy sigh. At least someone around here was relaxed and contented.

She wasn't too concerned that she might be arrested for something she hadn't done, though such things did happen. No, the disaster that loomed on her horizon scared her more than the off chance of an orange jumpsuit.

A murder case on top of a drug investigation was certain to expose Janice Swenson's blood ties to the Moran crime family. Did she dare hope the knowledge of her identity would go no further than the officers in the loop on the case? Or would the information leak and the news services have a heyday unearthing every rotting corpse buried in the basement of her heritage?

Most devastating—what would Shane think? The loss of his esteem would crush her.

Shane resisted the urge to fidget while Agent Durand studied the stone from the spot where the drugs were hidden. The DEA agent was actually handling the bulky item with gloved hands and was about to bag it in clear plastic.

"I don't mind telling you we've been after a smuggling ring operating through this area. I hope I'm holding a big break right here. We'll have to fingerprint you and Ms. Swenson for elimination purposes. You don't have any problem with that, do you?" The man's sharp gray eyes zeroed in on Shane's face.

If only his Adam's apple hadn't bobbed in reflex to the loaded question. "Can't say it'll be the most enjoyable thing I've ever done, but I'll cooperate."

It was hard to sound casual when a guy's nerves were strung tight as a guitar string about to snap. The fingerprinting business was going to expose Shane Gillum as Seth Grange. Paramedics' fingerprints were automatically in the system. How much discretion and understanding could he count on from the officers and agents involved in this mess?

Probably little to none, which meant he was about to become no better than roadkill in Janice's estimation. Strange that such a prospect bothered him worse than once again appearing on the Moran family's radar. Maybe their hired gun would shoot him quick and put him out of his misery.

"Do you think the murdered man on the beach is connected to the smuggling?" Shane asked.

The agent lifted a brow. "Too soon to say, but the question does present itself, doesn't it? What do you know about Ms. Swenson?"

If Shane were Atlas, his hackles would just have risen. "Enough to know she's as baffled and disturbed by all this as I am." Had he managed to keep the growl out of his tone?

Dry amusement flickered across the agent's face. Shane's spirits plummeted. No, he probably wasn't hiding any of his reactions from the sharp eyes of the law.

"She's not an old friend?" Durand's tone was mild.

"We didn't know each other prior to our meeting on the island this spring, if that's what you want to know. Any other information will have to come from her."

"Fair enough." Durand smiled, exposing a slight gap between his upper front teeth.

They went up the steep steps to the main floor, Durand cradling his treasure. "I'm going to have the local P.D. dust the surrounding stones for prints, as well."

In the hallway, Shane turned to the agent. "They should probably dust the north basement window casing on the west side. Somebody broke in through there. We discovered the break a couple of weeks ago when we thought we might be dealing with a mean prankster or some bored kids. We had the window repaired but you might still find prints in the area."

"What's this about a prankster?"

Shane filled in the agent on the string of strange events at the cottage, including the reason for the brace on Janice's wrist.

"Are you guys talking about me?" She appeared in the

doorway, crossed her arms and leaned a shoulder against the jamb.

"Mr. Gillum tells me the property was booby-trapped when you arrived on the premises."

She nodded. "We reported the incidents, and the officer took several articles into custody, but the initial assumption was random troublemakers taking advantage of a long-abandoned property. So there wasn't any kind of in-depth forensic examination. Our statements should be on file."

Agent Durand frowned. "I'll be following up with Chief Close. Thank you for your time."

Janice stepped aside and the agent headed for the front door, jaw jutting.

"You're not going to tell us to stay on the island?" Shane strode after him.

Janice's face turned a shade paler, but she didn't comment on his brashness. The agent turned, hand on the doorknob. Thunderclouds weighted his dark brows, but he squeezed out a cold-eyed smile.

"Is there any reason I should require that from you?"

Janice's answering laugh held a trace of a quiver, but she lifted her chin. "None whatsoever. Aside from our complete innocence, I have a job to do right here, and I'm not leaving until it's done. My only plans off-island include acting as matron of honor in my best friend's wedding in June. I'll gladly give you my contact information so I can remain available during that time."

Durand turned a questioning gaze on Shane.

"What she said." He shrugged. "I'm here for the duration, minus the wedding absence."

"I appreciate your willingness to cooperate," the agent said. "I'm issuing no such instruction and will caution the Vineyard P.D. about being too free with handing out restrictions."

"Thanks," Shane said.

The agent nodded and left.

Janice blew out a long breath that disturbed a strand of rich chestnut hair that had fallen out of her ponytail and onto her cheek. "Am I imagining things, or is the federal guy a mite peeved with the locals for going light on an investigation that now appears to be connected with drug smuggling and possibly murder?"

"You have an excellent imagination, but I don't believe you're exercising it right now."

"However—" Janice poked a finger at him "—methinks our friendly neighborhood DEA agent is a tad too accommodating to a pair of persons of interest like us."

Shane snickered. "Picked up on that, did you? Maybe he's hoping we'll relax and he can tail us when we go somewhere to meet up with our buddies in crime."

"In that case, maybe I'll see Agent Durand at the wedding. I hope he doesn't try to fingerprint the cake."

Shane burst out laughing, but quickly changed the sound into a cough. "I love your sense of humor, but I guess this is no laughing matter."

Janice's shoulders slumped and Shane kicked himself for letting go of the lighthearted moment. "Can we just bring in the furniture from the back of the Jeep and then grab those showers we talked about? I'll probably get a lot of reading done tonight, because I don't know how I'll manage to sleep a wink."

"What's the game plan for tomorrow?"

"Same as it's always been—keep on renovating the cottage. With more fingerprinting to be done down in that nasty cellar, at least we have an excuse to avoid tackling anything there for a while."

"So we keep on keeping on."

"Exactly right." Her expression changed. "How eerie to think you might have *seen* the shot that killed that poor man. I wonder what in the world a watercraft was doing off this beach in that kind of weather."

"In my experience, there are only two kinds of people who will take those kinds of chances. Crooks or heroes like the Coast Guard or firemen or—"

"Or paramedics." Her voice chimed in softly and her lips tilted upward, gaze alight with a look that thrilled and terrified him at the same time.

Shane melted in the warmth of her smile like a piece of chocolate basking in the sun.

Were they making a deadly mistake in remaining stubbornly in place at the cottage? Events kept escalating. Murder was about as serious as a situation could get. This time, the victim had been someone they barely knew, someone who was possibly involved in the smuggling of heroin.

What if next time the victim was Janice? Shane couldn't allow that to happen.

Even if he ceased his search for the records Dad swore were on the property, or if by some chance he succeeded in finding them, he couldn't leave Martha's Vineyard. His quest to wreak havoc on the Morans and clear his father had taken a backseat to doing whatever it took to protect this maddeningly stubborn, marvelously gutsy woman.

FOURTEEN

Then the bad guys were rounded up, the drug smuggling was ended—at least as it concerned Moran Cottage—and the insanity ceased. That was the mental litany Janice used to calm herself over the next two months whenever the sensation sneaked up on her that around the next corner something bad must lurk.

The murder of Moe had led to the arrest of Curly and the near-arrest of Larry, who was still at large but suspected of having left the country. Of course, those weren't the trio's real names, but Janice had picked up Shane's pseudonyms and her brain wouldn't discard them.

Who exactly shot Moe hadn't been 100 percent verified, but Curly claimed Larry had been furious with the jerk for recent carelessness. And, yes, others higher on the totem pole were involved in the smuggling operation, but the authorities had as yet to identify the ringleaders. Unfortunately, Janice was in full agreement with Shane's rather cynical assessment that it was often the "stooges" who took the fall, while the masterminds slunk into hiding, at least for a while.

Janice bucked her news phobia sufficiently to tune in to a couple of radio news broadcasts, and Shane filled her in on what local television stories contained. News anchors reported a number of details, but what they didn't report turned out to be the most comforting. They said little of either Shane or Janice. Shane seemed as glad about the omission as she was.

Which of the stooges was behind the "haunting" that nearly scared Janice out of her skin was guesswork, but hardly mattered at this point. Shane voiced some left-handed admiration of Larry as "gutsy" for being the one to point out the porch board had been chopped, not rotted, when the creep had been involved in the sabotage all along. To think that at the time, Shane had mentally praised the lumberyard employee for being an honest fellow!

After a while Janice and Shane ceased letting the recent danger dominate their conversation, and they found more cheerful things to talk about as they made fabulous strides on the cottage renovations. Shane wasn't as excited about their progress as Janice, but she could understand his low level of enthusiasm when he was meeting with nothing but frustration in his search for whatever Reggie Moran had hidden on the property. Even a foot-by-foot scrutiny of the acreage yielded no disturbed earth any more unusual than a rodent hole or an anthill.

At least Janice was able to leave the place in Shane's capable hands when she took off for the wedding in Denver. By June, tourist season was in full swing and getting anywhere on the island took two to three times as long. Now, while the aircraft began to descend on her return flight, she looked at Martha's Vineyard from her airplane window seat. Rays of the westering sun bathed land and ocean in a golden aura. It had been a long day of traveling and Janice could hardly wait to return to the property for some early shut-eye. Hopefully, Shane was already at the airport waiting for her.

Janice's stomach went buoyant as the plane swooped toward the runway. Were her anticipatory jitters about seeing Shane again? The man had thoroughly gotten under her skin, and Janice had found it a major challenge to hide her personal interest in him from her best friend these past couple of weeks. She probably hadn't succeeded if she'd correctly interpreted a few assessing stares Laurel had leveled at her the few times Janice had brought up Shane's name.

It was impossible not to mention the guy if she was going to give anyone the barest update on the progress of the cottage renovations. Shane had played a huge part in making it happen, especially after her tumble down the stairs. Not that she'd mentioned that incident to Laurel. The wrist was fine long before Janice's return to Denver, so why trouble the bride with tales of dangers past?

Besides, other than sharing that the property was on Martha's Vineyard, Janice had never told Laurel the name of the "distant relative" from whom she'd inherited it and didn't care to let too much idle chitchat change her friend's blissful ignorance that Janice could be listed in the Moran lineage. Such knowledge could easily lead to questions about her parents, and she simply wouldn't go there.

The plane's wheels bump-thumped onto terra firma and Janice placed her hands on the buckle of her seat belt, waiting for that pesky seat-belt light to be turned off by the pilot. Had Shane missed her? How could a person simultaneously love and hate such a thought? At this moment she might be exiting a plane to go greet him, but soon enough she would be boarding one with no prospect of seeing him ever again.

Impending separation wasn't something she could think about right now, she reminded herself. He'd discern her sorrow and ask about it. What could she possibly say that would make a speck of sense to him—short of confessing the unthinkable truth?

No, she needed to live in the *now* and take each day as it came. Dreading the future didn't put it off. A negative attitude just made life harder to enjoy today.

Janice stood decisively and fished her carry-on out of the overhead bin. Less than a minute later the line of people began to move toward the doors. Something about the back of a man's head caught her attention as she walked past. The guy was bent low as if looking for something under the seat ahead. Hadn't she seen that rather distinctive cowlick a couple of times during her sojourn away from the island?

Cowlicks were hardly rare, but this head of hair was particularly dark and bristly, and the cowlick did a near corkscrew in the midst of otherwise straight, neatly trimmed locks. If she wasn't mistaken, she'd seen the same unruly whorl on one of the waiters at the wedding. Then, as now, the guy seemed to be taking care not to let her see his face.

Spine prickling, Janice left the airplane. Was she being followed? At the time Moe's body had been found on the property, Shane and she had semiseriously discussed the possibility of a police tail, but after the arrest of one suspect and the escape of the other, they'd assumed the authorities were satisfied that she and Shane were not involved. What if they had assumed wrong?

Worse, what if this guy possibly following her wasn't with the cops? What if he was one of the crooks? Then again, why would any of the smugglers think it important to keep an eye on her? She had nothing they could possibly want, and they knew she wasn't involved in their racket. Nor was Shane. She was sure of that, wasn't she?

At a near trot, Janice beelined toward the baggage claim. Her heart rattled between her ribs like a skeleton in a cage. With a conscious effort, she slowed her steps. Way to look suspicious.

Warm relief cascaded over her as she burst into the baggage-claim area and spotted Shane standing near the carousel for her flight, hands in his jeans' pockets. He must have caught her approach from the corner of his eye because he straightened, grinned and waved.

His smile faded as she drew near. "What's up?" His gaze telegraphed concern.

"I could be paranoid, but I think I'm being followed... No, don't look." She squeezed his arm, noting the tense muscles beneath her fingers.

His face smoothed of its instant scowl and he desisted from turning his head this way and that. Only his eyes moved, scanning everyone who joined them at the carousel.

"Man or woman?"

"Man. He's got dark hair and this wild wisp of a cowlick at the crown of his head. That's what I noticed I'd seen before, including in Denver."

Shane clucked his tongue. "You've been followed the whole time you've been gone?"

"I think so, but getting off the plane is the first time I realized it."

He frowned. "I don't see anyone here like you describe, but I've been wondering about something out at the cottage. The same boat has been fishing parallel to your beach nearly every day since you've been gone, but I never see them haul in a net."

"What does all this mean?"

Shane shook his head. "I wish I knew. If it's the cops, I wonder what they're watching for. What do they expect might still happen out there?"

"And if the watchers aren't the cops?" Janice moved closer to him. "What if they're more members of the smuggling ring?"

Shane's lips thinned. "We'd better pray that's not the case."

Janice's lavender suitcase appeared. Shane grabbed it, and they hustled out to the Jeep. They got on the road, but progress was slow and a bit precarious with the number of two-wheeled scooters zipping in and out of traffic.

A scowl once again settled on Shane's features and he drummed his fingers against the steering wheel as they crawled along. "If that same fishing boat is out there tomorrow, I'm going to call the Coast Guard to check it out. As far as tonight, I hope you realize this means I'm not leaving you to sleep alone at the cottage."

Janice snorted a laugh. "I hope *you* remember that switching places with you doesn't do much good. People who do strange and scary things seem to know how to find me at your cabin, too."

"That's not where I was going with this. I've got a small tent. Atlas and I will camp outside."

Janice opened her mouth to speak.

"No argument," he said.

"I was just going to say thank you. Hopefully, I'm starting to learn to receive help graciously. Independence is my usual nature."

Shane's sidelong grin sent her pulse skittering.

"Nothing wrong with independence in healthy doses," he said. "You wear it well."

"Thank you." Did those words escape her mouth with a tone oddly like a purr? Not good that his approval meant the moon to her.

Dusk was upon them by the time they reached Moran Cottage. Janice had to admit the place looked handsome sporting a fresh paint job and some landscaping touches. Shane dropped her off with her luggage on the porch and then drove away to retrieve his tent.

Atlas leaped up from a snooze and greeted Janice with barks and licks and bumps against her legs that made her stagger. She shooed him back with an affectionate scold then followed up with a thorough ear scratch and released him from his long, outdoor chain. Wagging his tail, Atlas followed her inside all the way to her bedroom, where she deposited her suitcase and carry-on.

Janice gazed around. She'd furnished and decorated this area before she'd left, but she'd forgotten how nice this room looked staged with vintage furniture. The four-poster from the storage unit provided a striking focal point with its accompanying scalloped canopy and elegant tied-back drapes. Fortunately the bed was not from Clive Moran's era, or she would have had trouble getting to sleep in something she suspected he might have used.

"Come on, boy," she told Atlas. "Let's scope out the rest of the place. I hate to say it, but I've almost grown attached to this little cottage on the oceanfront."

Janice and the dog wandered from room to nearly finished room. The place was truly a beautiful marriage of vintage and modern. She should be elated with the achievement, but heaviness began to drape her shoulders. Shane had put some glossy touches on the woodwork and had finished the kitchen backsplash tile while she'd been gone. The new shower and bathroom fixtures had been installed by a local contractor. Final staging of furniture, window treatments and minimalist decorations were about the only details left undone.

All too soon she would be ready to list the property. Of course, she could put that off a bit longer if she wanted to spend time taming the acreage, but she'd determined that, aside from landscaping around the main building, she'd leave the rest wild. The new owner might want to add buildings to the property. For one thing, the place would make a lovely resort with room for many cabins, and then the ground would just get torn up. Or the owner might use the land for pasture, and in that case, wild would do just fine.

She stopped in front of the impressive stone fireplace and crossed her arms with a huff. A listing this well presented at the height of the season was likely to be snapped up quickly and at a premium price. Her depleted bank balance would rejoice, but would anything else in her world? It was no use pretending any longer that she was eager to sell the property and skedaddle.

Not without Shane.

But if the two of them had any chance at all, she would have to let him in on the truth about her—the whole truth that was so much darker than anything even her best friend knew about her. Dearest Karl hadn't known about her heritage. He hadn't needed to know. But Shane would find out. He'd put two and two together as soon as he met Laurel, and a few casual words from her would reveal Janice Swenson as the true heir of this property, not merely the Realtor. He'd see her roots were buried in a family he despised.

Would he still be able to love her? Assuming he returned her depth of feeling in the first place. Sometimes she thought he did. In unguarded moments, didn't she glimpse devotion in his eyes? Or was she deluded by wishful thinking?

On weighted feet, Janice returned to the bedroom and dug the old diary out of her carry-on. She'd been guarding this volume with her life, still processing it a few entries at a time. She was nearly finished. The situation wasn't looking good for Justine or for Gabriel.

The last entry Janice had read the evening before boarding the plane back to Martha's Vineyard was seared on her brain. Janice closed her eyes, and the flowing script appeared in her mind, deep black but backlit with a glow like the reflection of flames.

Father suspects I know what he's doing. His eye upon me is different now. Cold. Intense. Though he lavishes me with gifts and baubles, as usual, I am the enemy. What does he plan for me? Shall I warn Gabriel that his closeness to me might become a dan-

ger to him? How can I do so when such a word of caution would require me to fully explain its reason?

A high-pitched sound met Janice's ears and her eyes flew open. The sound had come from *her* throat.

Atlas whined, an echo of hers, and nudged Janice's leg with his nose.

"It's okay, buddy." She patted him and adjourned to a stuffed wing chair that she'd had re-covered in a floral print and placed in the corner. "I'll be okay." He settled on his haunches beside her and she stroked the animal's fur.

Would she be okay? If only life came with such guarantees.

Janice opened the diary to the spot she'd left off and removed the old newspaper clipping that marked her place. While in her renovated Queen Anne house in Denver, she'd climbed up on a chair and pulled down a small cask hidden on the top shelf of her bedroom closet. The cask hadn't been opened in more than a decade. She'd unlocked it and pulled out the yellowed newspaper article she now held in her hand. No need to open the folded paper. She could quote the awful text verbatim. The headline alone was enough to send her screaming. Literally.

Wouldn't she be a prize fool to bare this knowledge to the one man who had stirred her heart since Karl had left this life? If Shane learned the truth and rejected her because of her family identity, her heart would shatter. In his anger, he might even betray her birthright to the world.

But, a small voice murmured deep inside, *if you keep on hiding, your heart will harden and no love will ever again be given or received.*

Janice knew the voice of the Holy Spirit nudging her through her God-given conscience.

Not fair, God, she mentally protested.

Now she had to choose: protect the hard-won stability

of her life and what few trusted friendships she had forged. Or risk it on the off chance of gaining her second true love in this all-too-brief life.

"Justine, what did you decide?"

Janice stared at the diary, running her hands over the worn leather. Tonight, she would read through to the end. Would the generations-old words provide encouragement or leave her in despair? Or would the intimate narrative break off without resolution, leaving her nowhere? That was the outcome she feared most of all.

Shane flung the tent into the rear of the Jeep and slammed the hatch. He was so not in the mood for more shenanigans over at Moran Cottage. Did the heir have some kind of inkling what danger he or she had sent the Realtor into? If not, someone should have a heart-to-heart with the negligent crumb. If so, he or she had no excuse for sending an innocent person into harm's way—typical of a Moran—and Shane could cheerfully wring the person's neck.

Then again, about now he could probably cheerfully wring his own neck. He hadn't done a very stellar job at exposing any bad guys. His role in putting the cops on to the small fry in the drug smuggling operation had been negligible. Janice had been the key player in that regard. His grand plan to find the proof to send a gaggle of Morans to the slammer in his father's stead had turned into a major waste of time. Well, not entirely. He'd met Janice.

Lovely! Now this trip could spell heartbreak for him, as well as major heartache for his father.

The past fourteen days without Janice by his side had stretched into infinity. Now that she was home—if he could think of it as such—he longed to spend a quiet evening reconnecting. Their conversations had been fun and fascinating these past couple of months, covering a lot of ground about what sort of people they were, attitudes and life philosophies. The two of them absolutely clicked. Sure, she didn't know his real name or the identity of the person he was determined to exonerate, but then, she had a few Keep Off of Topic signs out there, too. When they were together, the omissions didn't seem to matter.

Frowning, Shane drove toward the Moran property. But what they hadn't said to each other *did* matter, at least on his part. If he couldn't be fully himself, a future together was doomed before it began.

He'd been thinking a lot about that reality while she'd been gone. The outcome of his quest to clear his father and rescue the family honor didn't look promising. Was it noble or ignoble of him to refuse to allow Janice the choice of whether she wanted to be with a felon's son or not?

The inner argument had raged long and hot. This afternoon, before she'd arrived, he'd decided to go for it. The worst that could happen was that she would walk away, which would be the same outcome if he didn't tell her the whole truth. The rejection might hurt worse than anything he'd experienced, but at least he wouldn't have to live with a gnawing sense of cowardice the rest of his life. And the lack of closure would likely drive him nutty. But now that the scent of danger had blown across their paths once more, any soul-baring would have to wait.

Shane cruised slowly up Janice's driveway. Pale light, such as what might come from a reading lamp, filtered through the blinds of the back bedroom, but light shone from nowhere else in the cottage. Janice must have decided to turn in early. He bottled his disappointment. No conversation tonight, but he couldn't blame her. She was probably all in. The trip from Denver to Martha's Vineyard took the best part of ten hours, even with only one layover.

So as not to disturb her with his headlamps, he clicked off his lights as he coasted into a parking spot next to her rental car. He shut off the Jeep but froze as his hand closed around the door latch. Had a muted glow flickered then winked out somewhere to the rear of the storage shed in the backyard?

Shane sat still, staring. The flicker was not repeated. He shook his head. A firefly maybe? Probably take several of them to create a glow that strong. On the other hand, wasn't a firefly glow likely to recur? On the other, other hand, he could be seeing things out of sheer jumpiness.

His chin firmed. Whatever it was, he was going to check it out. He'd rather laugh at himself tonight than kick himself in the morning if something hinky was going on back there.

If someone was there, he or she must have noticed his vehicle driving up. He needed to act naturally, as if he didn't suspect a thing.

Shane opened the Jeep's door, stepped out and headed for the porch of the cottage, as though he planned to go in the front door. Then he could cross the porch and sneak around to the back of the shed from the opposite side. Maybe he should actually go inside first, alert Janice and make a quick 9-1-1 call....

Biting his bottom lip, he climbed the front steps. Every shred of pride rebelled against sounding the alarm when it could well turn out to be false. He'd look foolish. Every protective instinct demanded that he take swift and accurate action, and that included exercising extreme precautions where Janice was concerned.

The decision was a no-brainer. Reaching for the knob, he strode toward the front door.

"Seth Grange."

The cold hiss halted him in his tracks. Every hair on his body prickled to attention.

"Daddy's golden boy." The voice slithered like a snake out of the dark. "Did you really think you were going to spoil my perfect record?"

FIFTEEN

Janice settled deeper into the pillow that rested against the headboard of her bed and flipped the page of Justine's diary. Few leaves remained to turn. The entries were becoming frantic—fierce even. Instead of fluid penmanship Janice worked to decipher quick scrawls. No more mundane reports regarding daily life. This was the account of a woman in crisis with pivotal choices to make.

The top of the fresh page began with terse verve.

I can keep silent no longer. If one more ship meets with disaster, it will be my fault. If one more sailor perishes who might have been saved, leaving behind a grieving widow and destitute children, the blood and the misery will be on my hands.

Love for my father has turned to loathing. Or perhaps the loathing is so strong because I yet love him.

Janice's windpipe thickened and she blinked away tears then plunged on in the narrative.

I continue to ask myself, does my mother know? Her health has always been so fragile, mentally as well as physically. Could her precarious state be due to a heart realization of the truth that she refuses to

*admit, even to herself? A part of me almost wishes
I could go there also—to that place of willful ignorance that dulls the pain. But I am not made that way.*

*Before I do the unthinkable and reveal the hor-
ror to those who can stop it, there is one to whom I
owe an explanation. In my weakness, I have allowed
our relationship to move beyond infatuation. Now
he must become privy—*

A sharp bark startled the diary out of Janice's hands.
The book flopped onto the covers. Atlas woofed again
and leaped up from the bedside rug. The dog trotted to
the closed bedroom door, nails clicking on the hardwood,
and whined.

"What is it, boy? Do you need to go out?"

Janice swung her pajama-clad legs over the side of the
bed. Punching her feet into a pair of mule slippers, she
grabbed her lightweight robe from the foot of the bed.
Atlas barked again.

"Okay, big guy. I'm coming."

Letting out a half laugh, half huff, she opened the bedroom door. Atlas lunged up the hallway and rounded the
corner into the main room. Janice shuffled along after him.

She stopped and stared around the sitting room. "Where
did you go?"

Normally the dog waited at the front door to be let out.
He wasn't there. A snuffling sound from the kitchen sent
Janice toward the side door in the kitchen.

She laughed. "You must be looking for Shane."

She'd heard his Jeep pull up on the gravel outside and
the slam of his vehicle door. He was probably setting up
his tent on this side of the house. The lawn was better
over here.

What a terrible hostess she was! She should have offered
to hold a flashlight or an electric lantern for him while he

worked in the near pitch dark. Then again, the guy was awfully self-sufficient. He would have thought about the light issue and rigged up a solution on his own.

Janice opened the door and the dog streaked outside. No jury-rigged light or shadowy activity in the dark betrayed Shane's presence. The yard was empty.

Where had Atlas gone? Of more vital importance, where was Shane?

A fierce growl from the rear of the cottage answered her question about the dog. A deep thud and a truncated yelp turned Janice's pulse into a roar in her ears. The outer darkness pressed upon her, thick and heavy. Instinct cried run, but her feet were nailed to the floor.

Run? Which way? Toward the sound where Atlas and certainly Shane were in trouble? Or slam and lock the door and race to the phone to call for help? Only the latter made good sense—for her and for them, but turning away from the door nearly wrenched her heart from her chest.

Breathing as if she'd sprinted up the steep incline from the beach to the cottage, she grabbed the telephone handset. The dial tone hummed then ceased as she punched in 9-1-1. The phone rang once, then twice, then—nothing. Stone silence told her the line was dead.

A blink later the lights in the cottage went out.

Janice's mind went as dark as the atmosphere around her. Her heart stalled then plunged into a gallop. Loss of phone line and electricity could only mean someone had cut the power. What should she do? It was logical to assume she was a target of the hostile presence. Where could she go? Her enemy could come through any window or break down a door. Or, if she fled out one egress or another, she might run straight into him.

Come on, girl! Think! There had to be a way of escape. The cellar!

She could climb down there and slip out the doors to the outside. From that point, her car was right around the corner. The best thing she could do for Shane and Atlas was to get away from here and find help.

Her eyes had somewhat adjusted to the darkness. She hurried out of the kitchen and through the sitting room, dodging furnishings half by memory, half by spotting darker silhouettes in the dimness.

The sound of a footfall on the porch spurred her faster, and she miscalculated, jabbing her toes against the leg of a high-backed armchair. Pain stabbed through her foot. Biting her lips to stifle a cry, she hobbled onward.

Behind her, window glass shattered. Beside her, the base of a lamp exploded, showering her with shards of ceramic. Janice darted into the hallway. What was that? Her mind struggled to make sense of the breakage. A bullet. Had to be. She'd heard no gun blast, but she would not necessarily have heard the spit of a silenced pistol.

Janice reached her bedroom and grabbed her purse from the top of the chest of drawers. Back in the hallway, clutching to her chest the vital container of her car keys, she groped at the floor with one hand for the entrance to the cellar.

Noises from the front door indicated someone attempting to get in.

God, please help me find— There!

Janice's fingers closed around the recessed latch and she heaved upward. Running on pure adrenaline, she propelled herself at foolish speed down the steep stairs into a black hole. She barely remembered to pull the trap door closed after her. Figuring out where she went ought to slow her pursuer.

At the base of the stairs, Janice fumbled in her purse for her cell phone. At last she pulled it out. The face lit and a pale glow bathed her immediate vicinity. Hand quivering, she found and pressed the flashlight button. A beam extended a bright finger into the darkness. As much as she'd despised the musty, dusty, useless space, at this moment it was a refuge. Janice inhaled a long breath and let it out slowly. She repeated the process several times until her jumbled insides settled back into an approximation of their proper places.

She'd need all the guts and savvy and speed she could muster to pull off her next move. Pointing the beam toward the cement steps, Janice hurried toward them. Her slippered feet made little scuffling noises on the packed earth.

Overhead, a crash sounded, followed by a thump and deep-voiced bellow. Janice grinned.

Welcome to my house. You're the stupid jerk who put out the lights and didn't bring a flashlight.

At least she now knew the location of the adversary. Emboldened, she quickly undid the inner latch on the doors to the outside. Putting her shoulder into it, she slowly raised one of the door panels. The protest of the rusty hinges echoed in her ears like a scream in the night. Janice winced. The noise was probably more like a whimper, but any sound at the moment was about a million times too loud.

The beam of her flashlight showed the coast was clear. She flung the door wide and let it flop to the side with a small clatter. Time to make a break for it.

Her dash toward the car was more like a scuttle, hunched low and digging in her purse for her car keys. Somewhere along the route, her phone slid out of her grip. No time to backtrack and retrieve it. She was at her vehicle now.

Gaze darting around for any sign of the intruder, she yanked the door open and flung herself inside. Three tries later, her shaking hand finally managed to jam the key into the ignition. The vehicle purred to a start. She threw it into gear and peeled out in reverse, flinging gravel under the carriage. The pop-pop-pop sounds, so much like gunshots, sent a shiver through her.

Was that a shout she heard from the field behind the house? Surely not. Had another engine just roared to life? *Please, no!*

Janice shifted gears and tromped on the accelerator. No headlights. Not yet. She'd make the highway by the gleam from the gravel beneath the meager moonlight. Lights would go on only when she reached the highway. Then she'd make a dash for Essie Mae's and a landline telephone that worked.

"Hang in there, girl," she encouraged herself under her breath. "You can make it."

Both hands strangled the steering wheel. Where was Shane? What had the creep done with him? A vision of Shane lying in a pool of his own blood tortured her mind's eye.

Shaking her head, Janice hauled her attention back to business. She couldn't dwell on distracting fears right now or she'd wind up paralyzed with grief that might have basis only in her imagination.

Yeah, right, a mean little voice taunted in her head. *You were shot at, somebody broke into the cottage, and there's no sign of the guy whose middle name is "protective." What do you think happened to him? Nothing good, that's for sure.*

"Shut! Up!" Janice hollered aloud.

Suddenly headlights flared on dead ahead, blinding her. She screamed and jerked the steering wheel to the side. The tires bumped onto the rough ground of the shallow ditch. A line of trees filled her sight and the nose of her car plowed into a looming trunk. The crash deafened her ears even as the airbag exploded into her body.

The bag deflated, leaving her coughing from chalky dust and hugging her bruised chest. Running into the tree physically might have hurt less.

Somebody yanked open the driver's-side door, unbuckled her seat belt and hauled her out of the car. Her legs had no strength and she promptly crumpled to the ground.

Burly arms wrapped around her waist and pulled her upright, but not with helpful intent.

"End of the line, Charlotte's daughter," said a bullish voice.

The bottom plummeted out of Janice's world. She was known! And by Officer Mitch. Shane had been right to mistrust the cops. Who else was in the loop?

Mitch dragged her toward—what do you know?—a dark-colored SUV. Someone in the back shoved open the rear door. Janice began to squirm and the arms around her tightened painfully.

The corrupt police officer shoved her into the backseat. Janice lunged toward the sliver of space between Officer Mitch and the edge of the door, but a hand buried itself in her hair and yanked her back. Cold metal pressed into her temple.

"Be still."

The subzero intensity in that voice quieted her as much as the gun to her head. She subsided, quivering in every limb.

Mitch climbed into the driver's seat and they cruised up the driveway, but didn't head for the parking area. Well back from the cottage, the SUV left the road and navigated the lumpy ground of the field behind the house, giving Janice's teeth a reason to chatter other than sheer terror. The SUV rolled to a stop behind the toolshed.

Their rotund chauffeur climbed out of the front seat and opened the back door. Without releasing his grip on her hair, her captor with the gun shoved her outside. They walked around to the front of the vehicle where the headlights illuminated the shabby rear boards of the shed.

What were they going to do? Line her up against the wall and execute her firing-squad style?

Mitch lifted an arm and pressed something under the eaves and the bottom of the wall began to tilt outward with a low, mechanical hum. The wall rose until it was completely horizontal above their heads and exposed a cavity of several feet between the false rear of the shed.

Again, Shane had been on the right track with his off-handed remark about the size of the shed. Too bad they hadn't investigated the small-seeming space rather than writing the impression off as an optical illusion due to the interior clutter.

A set of stairs led sideways down into an illuminated area below. The gunman let go of Janice's hair, but the muzzle of his pistol prodded her forward.

Gingerly, she set foot on the steep wooden steps. If only she could pull in a full breath, but it was as if an iron band encased her lungs. She glanced up and Mitch's grinning mug taunted her. He pointed down. She eased onto the next step. Could they hear her bones rattling together?

Attempting to swallow but not quite succeeding, she continued downward. More and more of the space below became visible. The size was double her two-car garage in Denver, but didn't quite match the volume of the cellar under the cottage. Apparently the space served as a warehouse of sorts. Rows of boxes and barrels lined one side of the room. A long, scarred table sat against the opposite wall, little white puff-packets strewed across its top.

A few feet away the big guy she and Shane thought of as Larry stood, straddle-legged and arms crossed, looming like a stone-faced Stooges clone above a crumpled and bloody figure on the floor. Horror thrust Janice to her knees.

"Shane!"

Janice's urgent cry penetrated Shane's semiconscious haze. His head throbbed, his gut burned, and every muscle ached, but he gathered himself and sat up. Someone let out a long groan. *Oh, yeah.* That was his voice. The ringing in his ears left him feeling detached from his body.

With supreme effort, he pried one swelling eye open a slit. Janice's beautiful face, framed by her glorious hair, gazed into his. The compassion of her stare sifted warmth through him.

"What have they done to you?" Her fingertips touched his swollen jaw.

Reflexively, his head turned and his lips brushed her palm. Color flushed her pale cheeks and her gaze slid away.

"It appears," he said, "that our friend Larry isn't merely a builder or just a saboteur. His true calling is prizefighter. Oh, and enforcer for the mob."

He'd meant to sound jaunty in spite of his wounds, but the words came out slurred as if he'd been hitting the bottle. His muscles and bones felt as though the bottle had been hitting him.

Janice's glare up at the husky Larry should have seared the guy's skin off. A bitter chuckle shook Shane's ribs and he winced into silence.

"Ain't that touchin'?" A familiar voice spoke from a corner of the room in the shadow of stacked crates. "I'd call it an ironic romance, eh? Useful maybe?"

Shane scowled. The shadow-figure had lurked there the whole time Officer Mitch and Norman Marks had held him up as a punching bag for Larry. At least he wasn't dead… yet. The Marks Man was impatient to shoot him and clear the disgrace from his reputation.

Did they want something from him first? What could it be? He'd been a complete bust as a secret-record sleuth.

The figure in the corner stepped into the light. Identity confirmed.

Janice gasped. "Mr. Beaseley? You're involved in this?"

The old fisherman displayed an affable, snaggle-toothed smile. "In it? I'm the only one standin' here that has half a brain."

Larry's scowl deepened and Mitch grunted.

"Be careful who you're calling dumb, pops." The hit man buffed the barrel of his pistol against his expensive polo shirt.

Beaseley narrowed his gaze on Norman. "Yer a gun for hire, and tops at your trade. Each to his own skills, ayuh. The Morans didn't trust me to run this slice of the business because I can shoot or punch or fix evidence at the cop shop, but because I can think. And now we have some loose ends to tie up delicate-like. You'll be takin' my directions if any of you want to keep on breathin' free air outside the pen."

Mutinous looks on the henchmen's faces didn't bode well for the fisherman's authority. Maybe Shane could use that crack in their armor to good advantage, if only he could figure out how.

Larry cracked the knuckles on his right hand. "That idea of booby-trapping the place to run off the heir worked real well, huh?"

"'Tweren't possible to anticipate uncommon stubbornness. You two—" Beaseley poked a finger toward Janice and Shane "—would have been sensible to take a hint, pack it up and go on home. But I'll give you this, young man, yer fast on your feet, even if yer not too smart, ayuh."

Beaseley squatted down on his haunches and looked Shane full in the eye, a sly grin creasing the wrinkles on his face. "Bet ya didn't know you've been workin' this whole summer long for the daughter of Charlotte Moran."

Shane's mouth went dry. The breath left him as if he'd been punched in the gut…again. Janice was a Moran? It couldn't be true. He wouldn't believe it.

The grin widened as the old fisherman turned his gaze on Janice. "Bet ya didn't know Shane's not Shane. Name's Seth Grange, son of Dexter Grange, Reggie Moran's bookkeeper and right-hand man in every scheme they floated. Bet Seth ran some cock-and-bull story past you 'bout huntin' for evidence to clear the innocent and expose the guilty. Ha!" At Janice's wide-eyed pallor, the guy chuckled. "Yep, see I hit that nail on the head. It's all about money, honey. Big money. Moran Family money."

"You lie!" Seth burst out. "There is no money! Never was. You're the dupes! None of it's true. Well, except the part about my name. My father *is* innocent. He was framed. And Janice is no Moran. She's the Realtor for the Moran heir."

Clicking his tongue, Beaseley rose to his feet.

Seth turned a desperate stare on Janice, both eyes opened as wide as they could against the swelling. She wouldn't meet his gaze. In fact, she rose slowly and turned her back on him. Seth's stomach curdled.

"May I please shoot my mark now?" Norman drawled as if asking permission to step out for a breath of fresh air.

"Don't git yer gills in a flap." Beaseley scowled. "Our business takes priority. Then you'll git yer chance."

"Yeah." Mitch stuffed his thumbs in his belt and puffed out his chest. "You still wouldn't have a clue to the location of Seth Grange if I hadn't ferretted out his true identity."

"You?" Larry snorted. "You couldn't spook a skunk out of a woodpile on your own. The DEA did your work for you, and as a courtesy, notified the local P.D. of the fingerprint match between Shane Gillum and Seth Grange."

Mitch stuck his face in Larry's. "You know this how?"

The boxer grinned. "I have my sources."

"You mean your Pattie patoutie." Mitch rounded on his fisherman boss. "I still don't get why the head honchos thought they needed to plant a second officer in the Martha's Vineyard P.D. I was doing just fine on my own."

"You want me to ask 'em to explain themselves?" Beaseley's tone was a kitten purr, his grin a Doberman's threat.

Mitch dropped his gaze and backed away, muttering under his breath.

The infighting among the gang members flowed around Seth like a chill tide. His mind was otherwise occupied, his gaze fixed on Janice's back. Her shoulders were slumped and her head drooped. Nothing like her usual elegant carriage. She looked crushed.

Why wouldn't she be? She'd been exposed as a deceiver. Typical Moran! A small inner voice reminded him that he hadn't been totally forthcoming, either. That was different, he mentally snapped back. His life had been on the line. Her motive was plain selfish pride. Of course it was. She was a Moran.

Janice's head came up and she turned on the bickering crooks. "Where's Atlas? What have you done with him?" She glared from one gangster to another.

The men gaped. He didn't blame them. That queenly ferocity was back and Seth's heart jigged in spite of his good sense.

Mitch's face turned a mottled red as he swaggered close to her. "I gave the pesky mutt a couple of good ones with this." He patted the nightstick at his belt. "Went down like a rock. Far as I know, he didn't get up."

Quicker than thought, Janice's hand flew and Mitch erupted into yelps and wheezing whines as he doubled over, clutching his face with both hands.

"My eyes!" he howled. "She put out my eyes!" Expletives dirtied the air.

Norman chuckled, Beaseley grinned and Larry's gaze on Janice turned admiring.

"Whoa, babe, that was awesome!"

Seth bottled a growl. The creep had stolen his line. He couldn't have put it better.

Despite the violent protest of his hurting body, he struggled to his feet. "Where did you learn that?"

Janice's shadowed gaze brushed his then fell away. "A

while back, I took a police self-defense course for civilians. Never used that move before, but I couldn't help myself."

"Enough!" Beaseley snapped. "Time's a wastin'. We got business to conclude."

"And then my business?" Norman ran his fingers down the barrel of his gun.

Seth's fists bunched. Buffing that gun barrel was an annoying habit. Could he get close enough to plant one on that fat nose?

Beaseley curled a lip at the contract killer. "You ain't long on patience, are ya?"

"Sure, I can be patient." Norman stepped back against the wall.

The fisherman gangster turned to Seth. "Sit down before you fall down."

Larry's burly hands grabbed Seth from behind and thrust him into a wooden chair. A groan gusted from him, but he sat still. No point in resisting. Yet. He pressed his tongue against an aching molar and tasted blood. Not surprising that a tooth had been knocked loose. Larry's fists were sledgehammers.

Beaseley leaned down and planted his weathered face in front of Seth's. "We're gonna have a frank conversation, and yer gonna tell us everything you know about the records that traitor Reggie stashed somewheres around here."

"I don't know anything. Haven't found anything, either."

"We'll see about that." Beaseley straightened.

The look he sent toward Janice dried up the last drop of saliva in Seth's mouth.

"You've had a taste of what Larry can do," Beaseley said, still eyeing Janice. "The guy's a pure artist at takin' people apart. Unless you want him to start on yer girlfriend, I suggest you recollect something good to share with us."

Seth's pulse hammered in his ears. What could he say?

He couldn't let anyone lay a hand on his Tuff girl. As much as he'd strive to protect any woman, his instinct to shield this one was magnified into infinity. She was a Moran, but God help him, he loved her whether she felt the same way about him or not.

"If you had this place—" Seth motioned around the underground hideout "—why did you need to stash drugs behind a stone in the cellar of the cottage?"

Surprise flickered in Beaseley's eyes, quickly followed by cold fury. Only the anger didn't seem to be directed at Seth or Janice.

"We didn't do that. There's a Luciano Family operator somewhere on the island. We've been workin' to flush him out for some time. Don't worry. We'll git 'im. He fried his own fritters when he tried to throw a monkey wrench into our operation by directin' DEA attention to this property. Bet he's plumb disappointed in the results. We're still goin' strong, and chances are he left some kind of evidence behind from his tomfoolery that will offer a clue to his identity. I expect the DEA will pass that information along as a courtesy to the local P.D."

"You have it all worked out, then." Seth lifted his chin as his right hand took a sturdy grip on the side of the chair.

He might not be able to prevail against the odds, but a chair whapped across Larry's skull should put the guy's fists out of commission. Protecting Janice was all that mattered now. They were likely to die in this place, but at least they'd go down swinging.

His dad? Well, Dad would hear eventually that his son was dead and, with the news, his hope of exoneration. Failure tasted bitter on Seth's tongue.

"We have to move this stuff." Beaseley waved at the stockpile of drugs and whatever contraband might be in the barrels and boxes. "We're a little behind schedule. But that's your fault, so the next words out of your mouth better be what we want to hear."

Seth told his body to shut up as he tensed his fiercely protesting muscles for action. But could he move fast enough to accomplish anything but getting himself shot?

At Seth's silence, Beaseley nodded to Larry. Licking his lips, the big man moved toward Janice.

"I might just have to steal me a kiss before I ruin that pretty mouth."

Pure red shot across Seth's vision and he lunged out of the chair, swinging it as he rocketed toward the stooge who went for Janice. Beaseley let out a bellow and Mitch yelped like a girl, still wiping at his streaming eyes. The chair met the side of Larry's head with a resounding crack. Grunting like a poleaxed bull, the prizefighter staggered and went down.

A fist of fire punched Seth's shoulder and flung him to the floor. The slight *pfft* sound that met his ears said Norman had entered the fray with his silenced pistol.

Seth lay still. Searing agony radiated from a spot under his collarbone throughout his whole body. His heart still beat, but for how long with his lifeblood pumping out onto the cement floor? The technicality was probably moot. In the next second or so he could count on a bullet to the brain that would spell lights out. Oddly, Seth felt no fear. Not for himself. Not for Janice, either, if they were fated to walk hand-in-hand into glory.

Norman let out a cackle. "'Bye, bye—"

"No!" The feminine shriek overlaid the hit man's farewell.

A warm body flung across Seth, multiplying his physical pain but sending his spirits into the clouds. She cared for him! If he could talk, he'd crow to the world that he was about to die happy.

SIXTEEN

A deep-throated blast reverberated through the enclosed space. Sharp cordite smell stained the air.

Janice cowered against Shane—er, Seth. Whatever his name was. She didn't care. Together, they were dead…or dying anyway. But where was the pain? And what was that blast anyway? Not Norman's silenced pistol. Had a bomb gone off?

Cautiously, Janice lifted her head. Not a soul in the room moved. Larry was still down for the count, thanks to Seth. Beaseley and Mitch stood stock-still, hands up as if fending off danger. Where was Norman? Her gaze slowly traveled the area then stalled at the table that had been strewn with drugs. The packets were still there, no doubt, but Norman sprawled on top of them, limp and still, the way a living person never could be.

Janice swallowed. The hit man had definitely been hit. More than once. But how…who?

Her gaze traveled on and transfixed on the bottom of the staircase.

"Essie Mae?"

How glad she was that the bulky female with a hairdo too big for anybody on the planet could move quietly as a cat. Who knew such a great server could also be a deadly shot? Of course, with a shotgun that size, it would be hard to miss anything she pointed it at.

The woman grinned darkly at the pair with their hands up. "You two don't move an inch."

"Now, Essie—"

"Not a word, either, Bill Beaseley, you snake." She jerked the shotgun in his direction. "If you think that broken windshield glass peppered ya, ya don't wanna see what the other barrel of this shotgun will do." Her gaze met Janice's. "You all right, lambkin?"

"Yes, I'm fine, but Shane... I mean Seth is hurt."

"Who? Never mind." Essie Mae shook her head. "See to your man, girl. I'll take care of these yahoos."

Janice turned her attention to the figure beneath her. He hadn't stirred in a while, but he breathed. *Thank you, God!* His eyes were closed, but maybe he couldn't open them for the swelling. His poor face! The rest of him probably wasn't in much better shape. If she could clobber that Larry guy again, she'd do it. And Seth had been shot, too!

She eased off him and he let out a soft groan. Blood had soaked the top left shoulder of his shirt, but at least it wasn't spurting. The bullet had missed the heart. Nor did his breathing gurgle, so in her uneducated opinion, the bullet had also missed the lung.

"Seth? Can you hear me? What should I be doing for you?"

The tip of his tongue poked out and flicked across bruised lips. "Make a compress for my shoulder, bind it up...and then could you drive me to the hospital?"

An utterly irrational gust of laughter puffed from her chest. Evidently, major relief made a person loopy. "It's about time I got to return the favor."

His valiant attempt to offer a smile looked incredibly painful.

"Hush," she said, placing a finger against his lips. "Let me take care of everything."

Ten minutes later Janice finished binding up Seth's gunshot wound with a towel and first-aid tape from a kit found among supplies in the underground bunker. It wasn't a professional job, but it would have to do. She'd even treated any other open wounds with antiseptic, much to Seth's teeth-gritted discomfort. Now he sat propped against a wall, head up, but face drained of all color.

Mitch, bloodshot eyes still weeping, and his boss, Bill Beaseley, sat in sullen silence, secured to chairs with duct tape. Apparently the crooks had been prepared for all kinds of emergencies in this underground bunker. Essie Mae had bound Larry, too, though he remained unconscious.

Janice rose from beside Seth and turned to Essie Mae, who was gazing around the room, eyes narrowed, cradling her shotgun like a baby.

"How did you know we were in trouble over here?" she asked the older woman.

"When Atlas showed up at my door limping like crazy and with a goose egg the size of an eagle egg on his noggin, I knew there had to be problems over here, so I hightailed it."

"Thank goodness Atlas is okay. Did you call the police before you headed over here?"

"Can't say that I did."

"That may be a good thing. Evidently, Officer Pat is in on this operation, too. We'd probably better place our call directly to that DEA Agent, Ed Durand."

Essie Mae pursed her lips. "That's good information about Pat. Not interested in callin' Ed. He's a straight ace. As annoyin' as it was havin' you two move in here, in the end, it's all played into my hands."

"What are you talking about?" Seth barked.

Essie Mae leveled her shotgun at them. "Sorry to inform you, but I'm not the cavalry."

The bottom dropped out of Janice's stomach. What was going on here?

Beaseley barked a laugh. "You're the Luciano plant?"

"Not a plant, you old goat. I've been here as long as you have. Reggie and I were…close. He'd been playin' two ends from the middle for a long time. *I* was supposed to be the heir to this place if somethin' happened to him. What possessed him to leave the property to Miss Prissyface, I have no idea. 'Cept he always did have this twisted sense of humor."

Beaseley grunted. "Like you say. He was playing two ends from the middle, and you got played, too."

Something like a soft whine came from Seth. "I suppose you've been laughing at us the whole time while we hunted for Reggie's records. I'll bet he didn't hide it here on the property. He gave them to you."

"I wish." Essie Mae sighed heavily, as if much put-upon. "He did come here, though, that last day. I musta been workin' at the time, but I found evidence in the field that a plane had landed. Didn't take but a week or so and the grass was all overgrown again. I figured he came to get something, not leave something. But it suits his sense of humor to start rumors about records that would incriminate everybody and their monkey's uncle."

"What about the money he was hiding from the rest of us?" Beaseley snapped.

"You have no idea how much!" Essie Mae rolled her eyes. "Clever didn't begin to describe Reggie, but I reckon the location of his private bank accounts died with him. He'd keep that sort of information up here." She tapped her head. "Chitchat time is over." Her glare moved to Janice. "You're the one that has what I'm lookin' for."

"I haven't found anything of value on this property."

Janice raised her chin. "Just heartache and more heart-ache."

"Don't play coy with me, lambkin. You found that old rascal Clive Moran's journal. I've been watchin' you from time to time in the evenings, sneakin' quick reads in that old book you brought back from the storage unit."

"You've been window-peeping?" Janice's mouth hung ajar and refused to close. She could scarcely draw a full breath. Why hadn't she felt that treacherous gaze on her? Shouldn't she have had the willies or something?

Essie Mae chuckled, rainbow-shadowed eyes twinkling. "Window-peeping, if you want to call it that. Window-scaring, too, at Shane's old cabin. Glad you weren't hurt bad or anything, but your young man was about to expose *my* stash of private documents, and I needed him out of there ASAP. It was rather a brainstorm to plant that packet of heroin instead, don't you think?"

"How did you get into the cottage to hide your things there?" Janice bit out her words. "You'd hardly fit through that broken window in the cellar."

"No, indeed." The woman chuckled. "But I never had to do anything but make it look like someone broke in. You see, I've always had a key to the place. That old fox, Reggie, gave me one years ago."

A deep moan drew Janice's head around. Seth was levering himself into a standing position with his good hand on the wall.

"You shouldn't move," Janice scolded. "You'll start bleeding again."

"I'm not going to sit here and let this old fraud talk down at me one more second."

"Old fraud!" Essie Mae huffed.

"I suppose you're the creep who was staring in the cottage window the first day Janice arrived."

"That would have been me," Beaseley said. "She

showed up at a really inconvenient time. I had to take cover down here."

Janice rubbed her eyes, shoulders slumping. A great weariness had stolen over her. So much intrigue and double cross. So little integrity. Even the man she'd come to trust implicitly wasn't who he'd said he was.

"I suppose that wraps up the mysteries," she said.

"Not at all, lambkin. I'm convinced that journal you found holds the clues to Clive's long-sought treasure, and I intend to be the one to lay hands on it. Now, if you'd be so kind as to run up to the cottage and collect it for me, I'll just stay here and keep an eye on Shane."

"Seth," he snapped.

"Whoever you are." Essie Mae turned her head toward Janice. "Mind you come straight back. No tricks, lambkin. You're on the clock. Two minutes, no more, or I might have to do some more damage to your young man."

"But the book isn't what you think!"

"No talk, just action." She jerked the shotgun toward the stairs.

Feeling as if she'd grown a third foot, Janice stumbled up the stairs. What could she possibly do to get them out of this fix? When Essie Mae discovered the book Janice had found wasn't what she expected, she'd no doubt blast her and Seth in a fit of rage.

Who was she fooling? Essie Mae was going to have to kill them no matter what.

The fire in Seth's bones had less to do with top-to-toe pain than consuming fury. If he were a torch, he'd be a pile of white ashes by now.

"Now I know firsthand the full meaning behind the words 'You're not going to get away with this.'"

Essie Mae tittered. "With those flashing blue eyes, it's no mystery what Janice sees in you. If it's any comfort, none of these folks will get away." She waved a hand at the captured mobsters.

Beaseley let out an audible growl and struggled against his bonds, scraping the chair legs across the floor. Mitch just whimpered. Essie Mae chuckled.

"Let me throw you a bone, Shane or Seth or whoever you are. The cops will find the shotgun with your fingerprints all over it. You'll be famous as the guy who put The Marks Man out of business. Lots of folks will throw a party in your name."

"So this Clive Moran left behind some hidden treasure?" Seth gritted the words out between his teeth.

"Local legend says so, but you won't find that in any history books."

"Just in whatever journal you claim Janice has found. What makes you so sure it's the one?"

"If there wasn't something big in it for her, why keep it a secret from everyone, including you?"

Seth had no answer. It looked like just another way Janice had been less than honest with him. *Was* she after something for herself—a Moran through and through? His gut rebelled at the idea, but his mind said maybe so. Essie Mae had sure fooled him. Why not Janice?

Why not give her the benefit of the doubt?

The question vibrated through him like a gong struck by a mallet. *She's a Moran.* His mental answer fell from his thoughts, limp and lame. The woman had done everything but uncreate herself to put distance between who she was and who her family was. A person out for Number One didn't throw herself on top of someone else to come between him and a bullet.

"Whatever secret Janice was keeping, it wasn't for selfish reasons."

"Thank you." The breathless words came from the stairway as footsteps pattered down.

Janice's warm gaze soaked through him, softening hard places. Everything in him rejoiced to see her. She looked glorious, regal even in pajamas, robe and slippers, crowned with a tousled mane of hair.

"Hand it over." Essie Mae's harsh demand destroyed the moment.

Janice thrust an ancient-looking leather book toward the woman. "Take it. I hope it makes you happy. I didn't even get to finish it to find out what happened."

"Find the directions to the treasure, you mean?"

"You figure it out." Chin up, Janice strode over to Seth and stood beside him. "I'm sorry. If I could have thought of a way to save us, I would have done it. No phone. No time."

Seth wrapped his good arm—well, his better arm—around her and pulled her close. "No apologies necessary. These have been among the most wonderful days of my life. The tensest, perhaps, but the best, too."

"Oddly enough, I feel the same way."

"Well, ain't that sweet?" Beaseley sneered. "Essie Mae, if you don't put these two out of their misery pronto, I may just puke."

"You keep a civil tongue in your head," she answered. "I've got my own way of doin' things, and you and Sleeping Beauty and Top Cop here are goin' first." She patted her shotgun. "Then I'm gonna pop those two with Norman's gun. It'll look like the shoot-out of the century. No survivors. I can see the tabloids now!"

Essie Mae radiated childlike glee as she bobbed up and down on pudgy feet, grinning like a maniac.

Movement on the stairs caught Seth's eye. A big canine head poked below the ceiling. The uncannily humanoid but extremely fuzzy face sent a look that fairly shouted, "May I join you?"

Seth drew himself away from the wall that had been propping him up. His legs would hold him…for how long, he didn't know. Janice's expression was shuttered, her focus on Essie Mae. He couldn't afford to alert her in any way. This was up to him, so he braced himself to move quickly. *God, help me!* This was going to hurt but the alternative was…well, stunning but premature. If possible, he'd postpone the gates of glory.

"Come on, boy!" he called.

The dog responded with a bark and a happy lunge down the steps. Essie Mae let out a squawk and wheeled around. Shane leaped forward. Two steps into his desperate lunge, his knees gave out. He extended himself for a tackle and reached her arm, ripping it away from the gun. Out of left field another figure hit the woman full-on with head and shoulder to the gut.

Essie Mae's outraged scream cut off into a high-pitched gag as she tumbled backward, Janice on top of her. The shotgun skittered away and disappeared under the drug table.

Atlas joined the fray, gleefully leaping on all and sundry, tongue busily licking every bit of exposed skin he could find on everyone present. Mitch's chair toppled then Beaseley's. Their helpless yowls joined the hubbub. Essie Mae rediscovered her voice and added soprano to the discordant symphony. Atlas anointed her face to the tune of blistering profanity Seth had never before heard from female lips.

He could only lie there, stretched out on the floor and battling the darkness that threatened to steal his consciousness. If he thought he was hurting before, that was a stubbed toe compared to a heart attack. He needed someone to put him out of his misery. Fast!

Oh, yeah, he could have had that taken care of if he'd let Essie Mae shoot them.

SEVENTEEN

Janice wandered from room to room in the cottage. In the main living area, she spotted Atlas snoozing on the rug in front of the empty hearth. A smile creased her lips. She'd let the hero of the hour sleep to his heart's content.

Much had been accomplished in the renovation of Moran Cottage, but a fair bit remained to do. She'd be on her own for the rest of the work—if she even had the heart to complete it. Each space had begun to be filled with delightful things, and yet each room felt oh-so-empty. So this was how desolate and forsaken felt.

Shane—no, Seth—was still in the hospital. Had been for the past two days and was slated for at least another overnight. She'd offered to have him stay at the cottage for a few more recovery days after that, but he'd very politely declined.

He was determined to return to New York since he was of no possible use around the cottage. Neither of them mentioned the obvious: that he had no more need to hide now that he'd given up his search for records that probably didn't exist, and the rest of the mob members were going to be scrambling to distance themselves from the fiasco on Martha's Vineyard.

Atlas would stay with Janice for the time being. Seth's apartment complex didn't allow pets. If and when he found new digs, he'd send for the dog. Maybe he'd even come get the animal. Janice's heart leaped at the thought, but she stilled the reaction. No use nursing forlorn hope for a couple of ships passing in the night.

Their relationship had become cordial. That was the best way Janice could describe the transition out of warmth and good humor to what they now had. They both tippy-toed around their new knowledge about each other. She could understand him changing his name and appearance and going into hiding from a contract killer. His presence at the cottage had put her at risk, but not any more than she had already been in for stepping ignorantly into the middle of mob business. She could also understand the drive to exonerate his father. That didn't look likely to happen, and Janice privately grieved for him.

What he thought about her true heritage went without saying. She appreciated his forbearance in avoiding all mention of the Moran name. Now that he knew her mother's identity, he had only to run an internet search on Charlotte Moran—one of those women who kept her maiden name even after marriage—in order to collect all the sordid details. That is, if he didn't remember the splashy case from fifteen years ago.

This new case at the cottage was hardly less splashy. A regular battalion of DEA agents, including the guy with the stand-out cowlick that she'd seen on the plane, had practically trampled the place, asking a ton of questions. The law *had* been following her around, though the boat Seth had seen for days offshore of the cottage turned out to have been Bill Beaseley's.

A contingent from the FBI had followed on the heels of the DEA as soon as the contraband boxes were opened and discovered to hold stolen technology. Then representatives of the Coast Guard dropped by to collect the casks, which were verified as a shipment of liquor from a merchant ship that had been reported lost at sea. The authorities now suspected outright piracy.

Janice opened the door to the walk-in pantry. She and

Seth had neglected this out-of-the-way closet in the renovation process. The canned goods that had clobbered her were still strewed on the floor. The top shelf still hung askew. Might as well tackle this simple project. How hard could it be to reinstall a shelf bracket?

After picking up the cans and tossing them into a garbage bag, she collected a hammer, a cordless drill, screws and anchors. A complete dweeb with tools she wasn't. Pretty soon she was ready to drill a new hole for the screw anchor. The fresh spot wasn't too far from the last screw hole. According to the stud finder, the screw that had fallen out couldn't have missed the stud by much.

Janice started the drill and pressed it to the spot. The drill bit punched through the drywall in a split second then ground to a screeching halt. What? She tried again. Same result. Some kind of obstruction in there that wasn't wood. How to get at it? She tapped her bottom lip with a finger.

She could saw through the drywall and open up the wall, but that would leave a hole to patch, perhaps a sizable one, depending on what she found. The better approach would probably be to remove the doorframe and take a look-see to identify the obstruction first. This particular doorframe wasn't original wood anyway, since much of the kitchen had been updated sometime in the fifties.

A little moaning and groaning from the nails and huffing and puffing from her and the frame was dismantled. Funny, the nails sticking out of the wood looked shiny and new. She shined a flashlight into the wall frame. Somebody had wedged a metal box into the space.

Janice's heart began to pound. Could this be what Seth had been looking for all these months? She reached in and wrestled the box free. Ignoring her skinned knuckles, she examined the steel tin. It was heavy. The metal was thick. Locked tight, of course, the box was too small to hold a paper record book. Whatever was inside rattled when the box was shaken. A memory stick?

A hammer to the lock popped the box open and verified her guess. She turned the flash drive around and around between her fingers. This had to be what Seth was looking for. A flash drive was contemporary technology. Only someone recently on the property, like Reggie Moran, could have planted it. Of course, Essie Mae claimed she had a key to the place, but her hiding spot was in the cellar.

Janice's laptop beckoned from the lovely new kitchen peninsula. No. She closed her fingers around the stick. She didn't have the right to read this first. That honor belonged to Seth.

Tomorrow, when she picked him up to take him to get his luggage at his cabin and then drop him at the airport, she would give the stick to him, along with a letter of explanation as to how she'd found it. Her going away present to him.

For his sake, she prayed that the contents would be all he'd ever dreamed of finding. If she wanted one thing for Seth, it was a happy life and a family of which he could be proud. He certainly couldn't have that with her, so goodbye was all she could rightfully say.

Seth gazed around the bedroom of the cabin in which he'd spent so little time. He adjusted the sling that stabilized his injured shoulder. Funny that he should feel homesick for the cottage up the beach that had cost such great trauma to so many people, present and past. Maybe he was homesick for the person who owned that cottage. He batted a hand in front of his face. He couldn't afford to think that way.

He was beyond tired, but his body was healing. The trip back to his apartment in New York would be tough, but he'd make it, and then he could rest. Sleep for days if he wanted. No one to bother him, to come up with new projects to tackle or to tease him. The thought hurt worse than his wounds.

Not even Atlas would be there with him. But Seth had already said his goodbyes to the big galoot. The worst parting was yet to come.

"Is everything ready to go?" Janice's sweet voice sounded in the hall.

She appeared in the doorway, blinking at him expectantly. Those lovely green eyes consumed him. Moran eyes. But her hair…

"Do you color it?" The question popped out of his mouth and then he wanted to slap himself.

She just smiled and lifted a chestnut lock from her shoulder. "You mean my hair? I'm not particularly fond of its natural shade. A bit too vivid for my more conservative realty clients."

"Then they're a stuffy bunch. I think…" He cleared his throat. "I think a person should feel free to be whoever she is."

"Thanks." Her smile warmed, but then her gaze dropped away. "Let's get you going then."

A short hour later they had navigated the island traffic and pulled up at the airport. Janice insisted on helping him with his luggage until he could get his bags checked in. She'd said so very little in the days since they'd nearly lost their lives, and she spoke even less today. He could conclude only that she couldn't wait to be rid of him—to put behind her every reminder of the trouble he'd caused her—as much as she wanted to unload that cottage. Who could blame her?

At the security clearance line, Seth took the handle of his rolling carry-on from her. "Thanks for everything, Tuff. I mean that."

Her smile was brave and polite. "Ditto to you…Shane." She spoke his fake name with a little of the old teasing light in her eyes. "Maybe you'll decide to take up a fresh career in carpentry when you get back home. I could provide a reference."

He chuckled. "I'm going to miss that offbeat sense of humor."

"Thank you. It means a lot that you'll miss something about me. Here." She thrust a thick envelope toward him.

He raised a hand. "No, I told you I wouldn't take a cent. I accepted the job you offered under false pretenses."

"It's not money, and it's important. Don't open the packet until you get home."

"Okay." He eyed the envelope then tucked it into his carry-on.

With a wave, she turned and headed toward the exit. His heart went with her, but the only gentlemanly thing to do was to let her walk away. Even if she still had feelings for him, he couldn't allow her to follow up on them. Her birth family had loaded enough sorrow on her plate. The last thing she'd want to do is to hook up with a guy carrying more of the same baggage.

Back in Denver, Janice shocked her friends by buying a television and eagerly following the news, both print and broadcast. One week passed, then two, then three, then the scoop of the century broke—the top echelon of the Moran crime family had been arrested, and it looked as if the charges were going to stick. Not a word about Dexter Grange, Seth's father.

Seth called that night. "You heard?" he asked.

"I did. The flash drive must have been a gold mine."

"In more ways than one. I think the Feds are shutting down about a gazillion dollars' worth of hidden bank accounts and freezing a ton of assets, not to mention following up leads that will keep the Morans busy in court for the next decade."

"Good." Janice's heart leaped. "When does your dad go free?"

"He doesn't." The words came out hard, flat.

"What are you talking about? This was the break that was going to—"

"My father was playing me."

"What?" The breath froze in her chest. He couldn't mean what she thought he meant.

"A bunch of the most incriminating documents on the drive were in my father's handwriting," Seth went on. "A few even bore his signature. He wasn't innocent at all. He just wanted me to find the drive and turn it over to him so he could pull strings from prison and get his hands on all that money Reggie had stashed away in offshore accounts. I wouldn't be surprised if he was planning a jail break so he could run off and enjoy the dough. He thought I'd be tickled to go with him. When I turned the drive over to the cops instead of him, he disowned me, and I'm fine with that!"

The bitter exclamation trailed off into silence.

"No, you're not," Janice said softly. "You're not fine with any of it, but you have to find a way to live with it. Let me tell you about my parents."

"You don't have to do that."

"You know?"

"Yes. It's not exactly hard to round up the details when you have the right name to research."

"I need to tell you about it, anyway. If you think Norman Marks was a despicable human being, my parents were worse. Contract killers, both of them, utterly without compunction. Actually, they loved their job. They murdered people and then came home and acted like normal folks. I didn't have a clue what they were up to until the TV news blindsided me with their arrests while I sat sharing popcorn with my dorm sisters at college. My heart shattered. I never watched news broadcasts after that. Weird phobia, huh? Wouldn't even own a television. Well, until recently when I was holding my breath to hear how you had turned out."

"I'm honored, I think."

Seth offered a gentle chuckle that spoke volumes of understanding. Something tight and hard softened and unfurled around Janice's heart.

"Let me finish my story. When my folks were caught and the truth came out, I began to see that what had passed for love in my house was twisted loyalty to an organization that trumped real family every time. The cops even found mementos of my parents' vile occupation—souvenirs from their victims—stashed in the basement. I was physically ill for days, realizing I'd called that house home and the people who buried their sick treasures beneath our feet mama and daddy."

Janice swallowed a lump that had thinned her voice. There was something cathartic about laying out the whole truth at long last to someone in a position to fully empathize. She plunged on with her tale.

"When my parents saw that I was horrified about what they had done for a living, my mother called me a weakling and my father took me off his visitation list. Dad was killed in a prison fight within a year. My mom is still serving life without parole. I haven't seen her since I was eighteen, and she's never attempted to contact me."

Seth let out a low whistle. "I can see why you were a bitter young woman for a while and why you maybe made some wrong turns at that time in your life, but I'm thankful the Lord arrested you."

"Me, too." A smile grew on Janice's face. "I like the way you put that. 'Arrested me.' The best kind of criminal apprehension. The debt's already been paid."

They laughed together. The sound was cleansing.

"Thanks for telling me your story," Seth said. "Makes me feel less alone."

"Me, too."

A gentle silence fell for several heartbeats and then Seth cleared his throat. "So how's our shared pet?"

"Atlas is out for a walk with my honorary niece who lives next door. I think we may have lost him to her, though I suspect her mother is glad he lives over here."

"Sounds like a good arrangement."

"It works. Say, I wanted to ask if…" Hesitation stole her voice.

"Ask what? Shoot! I'm listening."

She gulped down her misgivings. Time to go for it.

"I didn't sell the cottage."

"Really? Why not?"

"The place wasn't ready, and I didn't have the heart to keep working on it after you…after you left. I closed it up. So I was thinking. You know, if you're not super busy next spring about the time we met this year, maybe we could get together. I'll bet you'd be able to reserve that cabin you had, since it'll be off-season. I mean, if you'd still like to talk after we've given ourselves a while to heal and think about things. I'm not expecting you to work on the cottage, but…"

Dead air on the phone hammered hard on her ears.

"I think you're a very wise woman," Seth said at last. "And I wouldn't mind doing some more work on the place together."

"Okay, then." She went on quickly, "If you decide that's something you'd like to do—no obligation—I'll be walking on the beach between our places on the anniversary of our meeting. Same time even."

"Sounds good. Really good."

They said goodbye after that and Janice put a lid on her leaping heart. He hadn't promised he'd be there.

But he hadn't said he wouldn't.

EIGHTEEN

Seth paced in front of the striated boulder that marked the halfway point between his cabin and Janice's cottage. This had been her idea, but she could have changed her mind in the past eight months. Communication had been sporadic between them in all that time. He'd called twice to check on Atlas. At least, that had been his excuse. Then she'd called him when it became clear that Atlas had so thoroughly bonded with Janice's honorary niece that the dog had moved next door to live permanently.

Janice had asked if that was okay with Seth. What could he do but give his blessing? That special canine had more than earned the right to choose his master—or mistress, as the case may be.

After that, nothing. Three whole months now and no word whatsoever. She could scarcely know how often he'd practically had to chop his hand off to keep from reaching for the phone with her number in mind.

The early spring breeze from the Atlantic puffed his windbreaker and he hunched deeper into the jacket. In the sky, gulls screeched and wheeled. The salt air was brisk in his nostrils, frothy waves teased the soles of his tennis shoes and the sun's rays shot sparks off the blue water into his eyes. The seaside offered a glut to the senses, but the only thing he cared to feel was Janice close to him, and the only thing he wanted to see was her smile.

Seth stopped pacing, shoulders slumped. Who was he fooling? She wasn't coming. He squatted at the water's edge and tossed a pebble into the water.

"Hello, stranger."

He froze in the act of chucking another stone. *Please, God, don't let me be imagining things out of desperation.* Slowly, he set down the pebble, rose to his feet and turned.

Vivid green eyes sparkled at him. The straight, elegant nose, well-formed mouth, stubborn chin and dark brows— all were familiar—but they were framed by a wealth of hair the color of flame on a moonlit night. She stood with her hands in her sweatshirt pockets. Her grin brimmed with that elfin mischief that so took his breath away. She was every inch gorgeous. Even more so than he remembered. If he'd known how to talk, he'd suddenly forgotten the skill.

"My name is Janice Swenson," she said. "By physical birth I'm linked to the Moran family, but I really belong to the family of Jesus Christ. How about you?" She stuck out her right hand, inviting a shake.

Seth took in a quivering breath. "Pleased to meet you, Janice Swenson, daughter of God. I'm Seth Grange. My natural father is Dexter Grange, but my eternal Father is the same as yours."

He took her outstretched hand and pulled her into his arms. She went without an ounce of resistance. Burying his face in that glorious red hair, he squeezed her close and breathed in her scent of pure lilies and cleansing sea salt.

"We're family then," she whispered in her ear.

Chuckling, Seth drew back his head and gazed into her face. She smiled and he covered her lips with his. No kiss since the beginning of time could have rocked a man's world as much as this one.

EPILOGUE

One Year Later

In front of the beautifully decorated hearth in the sitting room of Moran Cottage, Janice stood facing Seth. Their hands were linked as the minister concluded his brief homily on the eternal bonds of love. They had decided to keep the cottage—renovated, redeemed and rededicated from its dark history.

Nearly a dozen guests, the most intimate friends of the bride and groom, had gathered to witness the ceremony. By the grins on their faces, a person might think a wedding had never made them so happy. The assumption might just be true. All knew Seth's and Janice's stories, and all were committed to support them through thick and thin. Not many couples could claim that of every guest at their wedding.

Even the canine member of the wedding party had proved his faithfulness. Atlas sported a sophisticated bow tie for a collar and sat, dignified and head high, at the front and to one side of Seth. He'd borne the rings to the hearth/ altar in a pouch strapped to his back. His almost-human face studied the proceedings intently, the canine version of a smile stretching his lips.

"Before we continue to the exchange of vows," the minister said, "the bride has asked me to read the concluding passages from an ancestress's diary." The man cleared his throat and spread the pages of the leather-bound book.

"'Today I have made a discovery that changes everything,'" he read. "'Even before I confessed, the man I love knew all of my dilemma. Indeed, his inner struggles have been the same as mine, because our fathers are in unholy covenant with each other. What freedom it brings to me at last to know that I am not alone in facing the unthinkable. How I treasure this love that no unwelcome heritage can defile.

"'We are in agreement, Gabriel and I. The evil must be exposed, and then we must turn our backs on it and walk away hand in hand.

"'If ever this diary is found, I pray that it will be taken up by a sympathetic soul in need of a word of comfort. Once the worst is faced and the hard choices are made, with God's help we have the power to transform our reputation and restore the heritage we leave our children. We have chosen this day who we will serve so that generations yet to come may live in the light.'"

The minister closed the book and lifted his gaze to the bride and groom. Moisture gleamed in the cleric's solemn eyes.

Seth's fingers tightened on Janice's and she gratefully returned the pressure. Neither bothered to restrain the tears that moistened their cheeks.

Ten minutes later, at the minister's invitation, Seth's firm lips fervently claimed hers. Then they turned, fingers twined, and faced their guests.

"Ladies and gentlemen," said the minister, "it is my great pleasure to present to you Mr. and Mrs. Seth Grange. May rivers of life flow from this union to all whose lives they touch."

Janice looked toward Seth. Had he asked the minister

to speak such a blessing? Her new husband's miniscule shrug denied the unspoken question. A small smile grew on Janice's face and Seth mirrored it.

They would take the blessing as God's personal word for them—a family creed to live by from this day forward.

* * * * *

Dear Reader,

Scripture describes our reputation—our "good name"—as a treasure worth more than gold or silver —Proverbs 22:1. Of course, that doesn't mean we should become enslaved to public opinion. Many poor decisions are based on a "what will people think" mentality. No, this wise advice is telling us to live a quality of life such that, when others think of us or hear our name spoken, they instantly associate us with good things such as integrity, honesty and kindness. Conversely, a "bad name" can cost us relationships, job opportunities, the positive regard of others and even personal self-esteem.

Our reputation can be affected, positively or negatively, not only by our own choices and actions, but by the choices and actions of those with whom we are associated. For instance, a child's rebellious ways can reflect poorly on the parents, or parents' reputations can negatively affect children's opportunities in life.

When I hear about heinous acts committed, certainly my sympathy is first and foremost with the victims and their families. But I also think about the perpetrators' families. What a blow their loved ones' awful choices have dealt them. Their lives are every bit as devastated as the families of the victims. How do decent people cope with the horrendous acts a loved one commits? How do they move on?

Out of compassion for these additional "victims" I wrote *Shake Down*. I hope you found the story edge-of-your-seat exciting, but I also hope you were moved with compassion for Janice and Shane—Seth. The next time you hear of an awful crime, please pray not only for the victims and their families, but also for the families of the perpetrators. They need your prayers.

I enjoy hearing from readers so feel free to contact me

through my web site at www.jillelizabethnelson.com. You can also connect with me on Facebook at www.facebook.com/JillElizabethNelson.Author.

Abundant Blessings,
Jill Elizabeth Nelson

Questions for Discussion

1. Shane/Seth and Janice are people with deep hurts and deep secrets. In your life experience do these two things often go hand-in-hand? Why or why not?

2. Shane's intentions toward whoever showed up at Moran Cottage were strictly personal—find what he needed and get out. Yet when confronted by Janice's need, his motives instantly became mixed and in some ways conflicted. How often do we enter situations with a particular purpose in mind and then find the motives of our hearts challenged by the real people with real feelings and needs that we encounter in the process? Can you give any examples?

3. Janice and Shane are instantly attracted to each other, but each has compelling reasons to resist the other. At first, the reasons are primarily selfish. What are those reasons?

4. As the story progresses, Janice and Shane continue to resist their attraction to one another. However, their reasons begin to change. Do their motivations toward each other grow more selfless over time? If so, why? Describe the progression.

5. Shane describes his family dynamics as strained and distant. Now that a crisis has come upon his father, what do you think motivates Shane to risk his life to help a dad with whom he's never been close?

6. Nearly everyone in the story has a hidden agenda.

Name a few of those motivations. Which was the most surprising to you and why?

7. Why would Janice find it cathartic to personally renovate the cottage and sell it?

8. Janice relates intensely to the dilemma of her ancestress, Justine. Why were Justine's words in her diary so challenging and yet therapeutic for Janice?

9. In what ways were Janice's and Justine's situations similar? In what ways were they different?

10. Did Janice and Justine find appropriate resolutions? What do their decisions say to us today in real life?

11. Do you understand what might have motivated Janice and Seth to hang on to the cottage in the end?

12. Why do you think it was so important to Janice and Seth to have as guests at their wedding only those who were fully aware of their sordid family histories?

13. How does a person go about "living down" the actions of his or her forebears? Or children? Or him- or herself? Discuss.

REQUEST YOUR FREE BOOKS!
2 FREE RIVETING INSPIRATIONAL NOVELS
PLUS 2 FREE MYSTERY GIFTS

Love Inspired.
SUSPENSE

YES! Please send me 2 FREE Love Inspired® Suspense novels and my 2 FREE mystery gifts (gifts are worth about $10). After receiving them, if I don't wish to receive any more books, I can return the shipping statement marked "cancel." If I don't cancel, I will receive 4 brand-new novels every month and be billed just $4.74 per book in the U.S. or $5.24 per book in Canada. That's a savings of at least 21% off the cover price. It's quite a bargain! Shipping and handling is just 50¢ per book in the U.S. and 75¢ per book in Canada.* I understand that accepting the 2 free books and gifts places me under no obligation to buy anything. I can always return a shipment and cancel at any time. Even if I never buy another book, the two free books and gifts are mine to keep forever.

123/323 IDN F5AC

Name _____ (PLEASE PRINT) _____

Address _____ Apt. # ____

City _____ State/Prov. _____ Zip/Postal Code ____

Signature (if under 18, a parent or guardian must sign)

Mail to the Harlequin® Reader Service:
IN U.S.A.: P.O. Box 1867, Buffalo, NY 14240-1867
IN CANADA: P.O. Box 609, Fort Erie, Ontario L2A 5X3

**Are you a current subscriber to Love Inspired Suspense books
and want to receive the larger-print edition?
Call 1-800-873-8635 or visit www.ReaderService.com.**

* Terms and prices subject to change without notice. Prices do not include applicable taxes. Sales tax applicable in N.Y. Canadian residents will be charged applicable taxes. Offer not valid in Quebec. This offer is limited to one order per household. Not valid for current subscribers to Love Inspired Suspense books. All orders subject to credit approval. Credit or debit balances in a customer's account(s) may be offset by any other outstanding balance owed by or to the customer. Please allow 4 to 6 weeks for delivery. Offer available while quantities last.

Your Privacy—The Harlequin® Reader Service is committed to protecting your privacy. Our Privacy Policy is available online at www.ReaderService.com or upon request from the Harlequin Reader Service.
We make a portion of our mailing list available to reputable third parties that offer products we believe may interest you. If you prefer that we not exchange your name with third parties, or if you wish to clarify or modify your communication preferences, please visit us at www.ReaderService.com/consumerchoice or write to us at Harlequin Reader Service Preference Service, P.O. Box 9062, Buffalo, NY 14269. Include your complete name and address.

LIS13R

"We used to count the stars at night, Jack. Remember that?"

Oh, he remembered, all right. They'd look skyward and watch each star appear, summer, winter, spring and fall, each season offering its own array, a blend of favorites. Until they'd become distracted by other things. Sweet things.

A sigh welled from somewhere deep within him, a quiet blooming of what could have been. "I remember."

They stared upward, side by side, watching the sunset fade to streaks of lilac and gray. Town lights began to appear north of the bridge, winking on earlier now that it was August. "How long are you here?"

Olivia faltered. "I'm not sure."

He turned to face her, puzzled.

"I'm between lives right now."

He raised an eyebrow, waiting for her to continue. She did, after drawn-out seconds, but didn't look at him. She kept her gaze up and out, watching the tree shadows darken and dim.

"I was married."

He'd heard she'd gotten married several years ago, but the "was" surprised him. He dropped his gaze to her left hand. No ring. No tan line that said a ring had been there this summer. A flicker that might be hope stirred in his chest, but entertaining those notions would get him nothing but trouble, so he blamed the strange feeling on the half-finished sandwich he'd wolfed down on the drive in.

You've eaten fast plenty of times before this and been fine. Just fine.

The reminder made him take a half step forward, just close enough to inhale the scent of sweet vanilla on her hair, her skin.

He shouldn't. He knew that. He knew it even as his hand reached for her hand, the left one bearing no man's ring, and that touch, the press of his fingers on hers, made the tiny flicker inside brighten just a little.

The surroundings, the trees, the thin-lit night and the sound of rushing water made him feel as if anything was possible, and he hadn't felt that way in a very long time. But here, with her?

He did. And it felt good.

Find out what else is going on in Jasper Gulch in HIS MONTANA SWEETHEART by Ruth Logan Herne, available August 2014 from Love Inspired®.

LIEXP0714

SPECIAL EXCERPT FROM

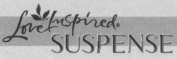

Love Inspired
SUSPENSE

*Someone doesn't want Sonya Daniels
to find out the truth about her past.
Read on for a preview of HER STOLEN PAST
by Lynette Eason from Love Inspired Suspense.*

Sonya Daniels heard the sharp crack and saw the woman jogging four feet in front of her stumble. Then fall.

Another crack.

Another woman cried out and hit the ground.

"Shooter! Get down! Get down!"

With a burst of horror, Sonya caught on. Someone was shooting at the joggers on the path. Terror froze her for a brief second. A second that saved her life as the bullet whizzed past her head and planted itself in the wooden bench next to her. If she'd been moving forward, she would be dead.

Frantic, she registered the screams of those in the park as she ran full-out, zigzagging her way to the concrete fountain just ahead.

Her only thought was shelter.

A bullet slammed into the dirt behind her and she dropped to roll next to the base of the fountain.

She looked up to find another young woman had beat her there. Terrified brown eyes stared at Sonya and she knew the woman saw her fear reflected back at her. Panting, Sonya listened for more shots.

None came.

And still they waited. Seconds turned into minutes.

"Is it over?" the woman finally whispered. "Is he gone?"

"I don't know," Sonya responded.

Screams still echoed around them. Wails and petrified cries of disbelief.

Sonya lifted her head slightly and looked back at the two women who'd fallen. They still lay on the path behind her.

Sirens sounded.

Sonya took a deep breath and scanned the area across the street. Slowly, she calmed and gained control of her pounding pulse.

Her mind clicked through the shots fired. Two hit the women running in front of her. Her stomach cramped at the thought that she should have been the third victim. She glanced at the bench. The bullet hole stared back. It had dug a groove slanted and angled.

Heart in her throat, Sonya darted to the nearest woman, who lay about ten yards away from her. Expecting a bullet to slam into her at any moment, she felt for a pulse.

When Sonya turns to Detective Brandon Hayes
for help, can he protect her without both of them
losing their hearts?
Pick up HER STOLEN PAST to find out.

Available August 2014
wherever Love Inspired books are sold.

LISEXP0714

Love Inspired® SUSPENSE

RIVETING INSPIRATIONAL ROMANCE

Emma Landers has amnesia. Problem is, she can't remember how she got it, why she's injured or why someone wants to hurt her. When she lands on the doorstep of former love Travis Wright, she can barely remember their past history. But she knows she can trust him to protect her. The handsome farmer was heartbroken when Emma left him for the big city. But there's no way he can send her away when gunshots start flying. Now Travis must keep Emma safe while helping her piece together her memories—before it's too late.

A TRACE OF MEMORY
by
VALERIE HANSEN

THE DEFENDERS

Protecting children in need

Available August 2014 wherever
Love Inspired books and ebooks are sold.

LI44613